Grace in Moonlight

Stephanie Julian

Ellora's Cave
Romantica®
ELLORASCAVE.COM

An Ellora's Cave Publication

www.ellorascave.com

Grace in Moonlight

ISBN 9781419953637

Edited by Grace Bradley.
Cover design by Dar Albert
Electronic book publication July 2011
Trade paperback publication 2014

Glossary

Arus: magical power inherent in the *Fata* and *Enu*, races of Etruscan descent

Boschetta: Etruscan coven, traditionally comprised of thirteen *streghe*

Candela: Etruscan sprite, tiny magical beings with wings and a certain glow about them

Decurio: legion rank of commander

Eteri (pl. *eteri*): Etruscan for foreigner, used to describe regular humans without magic

Enu: humans of magical Etruscan descent

Fata: elemental beings of magical Etruscan descent

Folletta (pl. *folletti*): Etruscan female fairy

Linchetto (pl. *linchetti*): Etruscan night elf

Malandante: descended from the Etruscans but born with a bent toward evil, with a taste for power and wealth

Praenuntio: Goddess Gift of foresight

Praepositus: an officer rank in the *lucani* army

Praetorian: elite guard of the *lucani* king

Pugio: a Roman dagger

Quercioli: the offspring of a *folletta* and a *linchetto*, always female

Salbinelli: Etruscan satyr

Sicari (pl: *sicarii*): assassin

Silvani: one of the three original Etruscan *Fata*; always female, protectors of fields and forests

Speculator: spy

Strega (pl. *streghe*): Etruscan witch

Versipellis (pl. *versipelli*): literally "skin shifter"—shapeshifters including Etruscan *Lucani* (wolves), Norse *Berkserkir* (bears) and French *loup garou* (wolves)

Chapter One

"No, absolutely not. I don't care what you say, there's no way I'm going to allow you—"

"Allow? *Allow!* Lady, you're not in any fucking position to allow anything."

"Don't you swear at me, Kaisie Giliati. And I don't think you understand. I will *not* allow you to go without me to rescue my son. He *needs* me there. He needs his mother. I'm all he's got and I will *not* let you leave me behind."

"*Non rompermi le palle.* You're just going to get in the way and I can't—"

"Get in the way! Ooh, you are *such* a jackass. Don't even *think* you can—"

"How long have they been at this?" Catene Rossini Ferante whispered the words as the two combatants continued, but Kaine Giliati heard them loud and clear.

Without taking her gaze away from the seething emotion between her father, Kaisie Giliati, and Grace Bellasario, she motioned for Cat to come closer. She didn't want to interrupt the battle.

"About half an hour," Kaine whispered back. "They're starting to circle back to where they started, though, so I assume Dad's going to storm out in another minute. That's the normal course of events."

Cat shook her head, careful to keep it subdued so she didn't draw Grace's or Kaisie's attention. "I don't know why your dad keeps fighting her about this. She's right. The team needs her help. She may not have a lot of power but she knows how the *Mal* do things. She'll be able to answer questions no one else can."

Kaine agreed. Silently. Her dad needed to suck up his objections and get with the program to take Grace along on the dangerous mission to rescue Grace's ten-year-old son, Alex.

A week ago, Ettore Marrucini had magically transported himself and six other men into the *lucani* den and walked out with Cat, Evie Simmons and Alex. Cat and Evie had gotten away.

Marrucini still had Alex. But there was no way the *lucani* would allow the *Malandante* to corrupt sweet little Alex and turn him into a monster, like the other *Mal*.

The Etruscan wolf shifters didn't hold Grace's sins against her son.

Hell, most people had forgiven Grace's sins, including the two women who had absolutely no reason to ever forgive her. But Tamra Macmillan and Evie Simmons had found a way to get beyond the fact that Grace had tried to kidnap Tam and had actually succeeded in kidnapping Evie and her brother, John.

For weeks, Grace had made Evie's and John's lives hell, holding them against their will while Grace had taken pints of Evie's blood on a regular basis. To create a serum that allowed her son to live.

Turns out Evie's blood had magical properties the *streghe* and the *lucani* medical doctors were still trying to figure out. The Etruscan witches had made some progress in determining that Evie's blood chemistry had been altered in some strange way, though not by Grace.

Grace had only been able to identify the fact that Evie's blood was different and use it to help her son. The hint of magic in her blood, something many *eteri* had but never realized, kept Grace's son from succumbing to a disease that wanted to waste the little boy away to nothing.

"Gods damn it." Kaisie's voice had reached almost to shouting level. "You're not strong enough to be of any help whatsoever—"

"And you're an ass if you seriously believe you can—"

Kaine and Cat exchanged raised eyebrows as the fight raged on but neither had anything else to say.

Ultimately, it wasn't Grace or Kaisie who made the final decision about Grace accompanying the team. It was Kyle Rossini. And Kyle, as head of the *sicarii*, the *lucani* king's assassins, had already made his decision. He'd told the four members of his team, which included Kaine, that Grace was going.

"You know what?" Kaisie finally threw his hands in the air. "I can't talk to you. You're irrational."

Kaine took a deep breath. Her dad had just reached his breaking point. When he started talking with his hands, she knew it was only a matter of minutes before he stormed out.

"I'm irrational?" Grace fired back. "You're the one acting like a madman."

And he looked like one, too, Kaine thought.

Anyone who didn't know Kaisie would think he was homeless and off his meds.

His dirt-brown hair hung below his shoulders in a straggly mess. It was clean but it definitely looked as if he'd been the one to butcher his hair last. Without the benefit of a mirror. His beard looked a little better than it had when he'd first shown up two weeks ago. At least he'd trimmed it down to a manageable scruff, which he would eventually shave off. He always did.

Six-foot and nearly two-hundred pounds of lean muscle, Kaisie had bright-green eyes a shade lighter than her own. They burned when he was furious, like he was now.

He'd never act on that anger, not in any way. Her dad didn't hit. If he was in his pelt and you were a mortal enemy, he'd fight until his last breath and he'd win. And if he could, he'd leave his opponent alive.

Still, he had an air of danger that gave him an edge. One that either made women run in the opposite direction or drew them like flies, not that he'd ever kept one around for longer than a few weeks.

Neither variety usually wanted to fight with him. And that's all he and Grace did until her dad decided he'd had enough and left.

She loved her dad dearly but the man had a serious commitment problem. Sure, he'd reared her from the time she was a baby and her mother had died. But more often than not, he'd left her with whatever family agreed to care for her that week when he went on assignment for the king.

She'd never doubted his love but ever since she'd been old enough to take care of herself, he'd been on assignment more often than he'd been home because her dad was the best tracker the *lucani* had ever had. If it was lost, Kaisie Giliati could find it.

It'd taken him less than a week to find Alex. Her dad was that good.

And now it was up to Kaine's boss, Kyle, to come up with a plan to get Alex out of a secure compound in Florida where Marrucini had stashed the boy.

Cat leaned closer to Kaine. "Do you think they realize they're hot for each other?"

Kaine winced and shot Cat a disgruntled glare. "Come on, Cat. He's my dad. Eww. Just…no."

Cat merely raised her eyebrows and gave her a wicked grin, to which Kaine responded with rolled eyes.

Hell, everyone in the *lucani* den saw what was going on between her dad and Grace. Trying to ignore the situation wouldn't make it go away.

And Kaine had to admit she kind of liked the woman.

Grace had done some bad things, yes, but she'd done them to save her child. No *lucani* would ever fault someone for trying to save the life of their child.

The problem was some of the *lucani* would never see Grace as anything other than a pawn of the *Malandante*.

The *Mal* were born evil and grew up to be monsters. They craved power and money and had no soul. They didn't love. Family was a tool to be used in the pursuit of power and domination. They had no friends, only allies. And usually they double-crossed those.

The *lucani* and the *Mal* had been enemies since the time of their creation. The *Mal* didn't mingle with the rest of the Etruscan race. They were a cult unto themselves.

And her dad had the serious hots for a woman who'd been reared by that evil.

Kaine sighed. She allowed herself a brief, selfish moment to wish Grace had taken Cole's offer to leave and return to the *Mal*, to retrieve her son by giving herself back to the man who'd ripped Grace's first-born child, a daughter, from her arms at the moment of her birth and had kidnapped Alex only last week.

Grace hadn't hesitated. She'd begged Cole to get her son back. She'd promised her eternal servitude. Hell, she'd practically offered up her own life for the *lucani* king's help.

Grace wasn't begging now. No, she was reading Kaisie the riot act for trying to force her to stay here at the den while Kaine's team went after Alex.

"You know," Cat whispered. "They'll make adorable babies. Maybe you'll finally have that sister you always wanted."

Even though she knew Cat was teasing, Kaine had a momentary flash of her father holding a red-haired baby in his arms.

She didn't shudder at the thought.

Turning to Cat, she raised her eyebrows. "Maybe it'll be a boy."

Cat's eyes widened just before she started to giggle.

And Grace and Kaisie broke off their argument to stare at the girls, as if they'd only just noticed their presence in the small meeting room in the den's community center.

"Kaine," her father practically barked at her. "Talk some sense into this woman. She's got less than a fly at this point."

Vaffanculo. Sometimes her dad really was an ass. Sighing, she opened her mouth to apologize to Grace for him but never had the chance.

Grace got right in Kaisie's face, her milk-pale skin suffused with a dark flush almost the same color as her wavy, auburn hair.

At thirty-five, Grace looked almost a decade younger, her rounded body completely feminine, her features sharp and pointed and her brown eyes the color of dark chocolate.

You couldn't call Grace pretty. No, she had more of a classical beauty, something you'd see on a marble statue in a Roman museum. Aristocratic. Regal.

Especially when she had that aristocratic nose stuck in the air. "And you are an arrogant, mule-headed *idiot* who has no idea how to see beyond his own ingrained prejudices."

With that parting shot, Grace turned and stalked out of the room.

Score one for Grace, Kaine thought. Usually her dad left first.

Beside her, she felt Cat still as Kaisie stared at the door Grace had left through. He almost looked as if he wanted to go after her. Frustration showed in the tight line of his mouth and the clenched hands at his sides.

Kaine had the unfamiliar urge to comfort her dad, something she never would've thought to do before. He'd always been so strong, so controlled. He had a reputation for being a loner, uncomfortable around other people, magical or not. He didn't work well with others, which Kaine had always attributed to being a tracker.

She'd had the same tendencies until she'd joined the *sicarii* and learned to rely on Kyle, Duke and Nic as her partners. And fallen in love with John Simmons.

Now she realized how lonely she'd been.

And she wondered if maybe her dad—

"*Vaffanculo*, that woman is going to be the death of me."

She heard the rough growl in his tone, the utter frustration she hadn't heard in her dad's voice since she'd been a little girl begging him to let her come with him on his frequent trips. She hadn't understood then that he couldn't take her but she'd learned not to ask after the fifth or sixth time he'd left her in tears at the home of one of the other *lucani* families.

With a sigh, Kaine walked over to stand next to him. "Dad..."

He didn't look at her right away. She could tell he was trying to control his temper.

When he finally had that slow-burning anger under wraps, he flashed a smile and bent to press a kiss to her head. She felt about twelve years old when he did that and she adored him for it.

"I know what you're going to say, little girl, so don't bother." Then he flashed a smile at Cat, who answered with a hero-worshipping smile of her own. "And how's my pretty Cat?"

Kaine rolled her eyes as he used Cat's adoration to deflect the conversation. Something else he was good at.

"I'm good, Kaisie." Cat practically skipped over to give her dad a hug, the girl's smile so bright it had to hurt. "It's so great to see you."

Hugging Kaine closer, he wrapped an arm around Cat's shoulders then steered them all toward the front door of the center.

"Good to be seen, sweetheart. Good to be home."

Kaine heard something in her dad's voice she hadn't before. Weariness.

She realized she hadn't known where he'd been before he'd arrived at the den two weeks ago to find Alex. With everything going on, she hadn't even thought to ask. Maybe he wouldn't even be able to tell her but she always, always, *always* asked. It let him know she thought about him. Cared about where he was and what he was doing.

Though the village had helped to raise her, she was and always would be a daddy's girl.

"Dad… Is everything okay?"

He didn't answer right away and that made her heart race as fear dropped into her system.

"Dad—"

"Everything's fine, sweetheart." He smiled down at her, though she still saw strain in the lines around his eyes and his mouth. "Everything's fine."

* * * * *

"Tinia's teat, what a fucking mess."

"I don't know what you're so pissed off about, Kaisie. It's not like you have to babysit the woman. Hell, you don't even have to go along to retrieve the boy if you don't want to. You found him. Let the *sicarii* handle the rest."

Kaisie threw Dorian Pellegrino a vicious look as he took a long pull on the beer she'd set in front of him before dropping into a chair at the dining room table.

"Grace Bellasario is a menace. And my daughter's normally good judgment seems to have deserted her when it comes to that woman."

Leaning back in her chair, Dorian gave him a long, steady stare. Years younger than his own forty-four, the *praetorian* was tough, smart and one of his best friends. Of which he didn't have many.

And most of them were sitting at this table.

Dorian sat across from him, her brown hair and eyes so perfectly ordinary but her face so delicately not. Not that he'd ever say that to her. As one of the *lucani* king's elite guards, she could toss a knife through a period on a magazine page from fifty yards and she could take down a warrior twice her size in hand-to-hand combat.

"Your daughter isn't the one who's lost her common sense." Dorian's eyebrows lifted slightly. "You seem to be spending an awful lot of time with the woman yourself."

To his left, Aule Pastore snorted as he pretended to check out his card hand. Aule had a wife and two kids, a slight potbelly from eating too much of his wife's delicious homemade pasta and had lost most of his hair sometime around the age of twenty-eight, nearly two decades ago. In his pelt, the guy was a stealthy predator but in real life, he worked numbers as if they were a symphony.

Kaisie frowned at Aule. "What the hell was that for?"

To his right, Jimmy Domenico started to laugh. "Really? You really gonna play it that way?"

Kaisie turned to give Jimmy the finger but the short, stout *praepositus* of the *lucani* army, the man in charge of teaching young soldiers how to be good soldiers, just laughed again. Nearly sixty and still able to best boys decades younger in a fight, Jimmy had a wicked sense of humor that, embarrassingly enough, included a love of Jerry Lewis.

"Now, boys and girls, let's not get into a pissing match. Are we gonna play cards or not?"

The horned *salbinelli* sitting between Aule and Dorian had a cigar clamped between his teeth and sat on a specially made chair so he was at the right height to play. Beneath the table,

Kaisie knew Salvatorus' goat legs dangled inches from the floor while his human upper body was all that showed above.

Sal flashed a warning look at Jimmy, whose grin only got bigger.

Son of a bitch. He'd joined the game tonight in Dorian's small cottage in the den because he'd wanted one night to just relax, drink a few beers, play a few hands and forget about the bullshit waiting to come down on his head.

Not to be badgered by his so-called friends.

The floating game had been going on for years, since he and Aule had been teenagers serving the first of their four mandatory years in the *lucani* legion. Over the years, players had come and gone but there was always a game somewhere in the den come Thursday night.

"I'm playing, I'm playing." Jimmy took another look at his cards then threw in a couple of chips. "But Kaisie, come on, man. Give the woman a break already. The bastard took her kid. She's allowed to be a bitch until she gets him back."

For some reason, hearing Jimmy call Grace a bitch put his back up. Which was ridiculous, considering what he thought of the woman himself.

Not that he thought she was a bitch. She was just…

Stubborn. Willful. Demanding.

Terrified for her son.

And so fucking beautiful she made his gut hurt.

So of course, he had to pick a fight with her every chance he got.

"For fuck's sake, Kaisie, if you're not gonna pay attention, just fold and put the rest of us out of your misery." Aule shook his head though he had a grin playing around the edges of his mouth, same as Jimmy. "You've won enough hands anyway. Give the rest of us a chance to win some money."

"Well, you ain't winning mine." Sal laid out a royal flush. "Read 'em and weep, children."

As the rest of the table threw their cards down in disgust while calling Sal's parentage into question in various and creative ways, Kaisie rose from the table with a sigh. "Deal me out next hand. I need a fresh one. Anybody else?"

No one else took him up on his offer, probably because he was sucking back beers like a teenager at his first party. And he still didn't have enough of a buzz to feel better about what had happened earlier.

Making his way to the kitchen, he opened the fridge, pulled out a beer…and sighed as he shut the door.

"No, Aule." Kaisie turned to face his oldest and closest friend, who'd followed him from the other room. "I don't wanna talk about it."

"Well, shit. I didn't know you'd become a mind reader." Aule leaned back against the stove, arms crossed over his chest. "And I didn't even ask the question, *scassacazzo*."

Kaisie shrugged. "Well, you were gonna. I'm just saving you the trouble of trying and failing. So you drew the short straw, huh?"

"No, I volunteered to come after you. We considered sending Dorian… You know, a woman's touch and all. But then Dorian's about as cuddly as an iguana."

"Whereas you're just a bundle of soft and fuzzy."

Aule patted his stomach with a rueful grin. "Well, you got the soft right. At least I don't have Jimmy's back hair."

Kaisie tried to give Aule the smile he was after but couldn't quite make it stick.

Instead, he sighed and Aule's expression transformed with concern.

"Hey, man. You wanna tell me what's really going on? The last couple of times I've seen you, you haven't seemed…"

Kaisie forced himself to maintain eye contact. "Haven't seemed what?"

Aule took a deep breath and shook his head. "You seem kind of close to the wolf, my friend. Like maybe you're spending a little too much time in your pelt."

Kaisie didn't bother to deny it. He couldn't.

"What's going on?" Aule leaned forward, his voice dropping to barely a whisper. "Kaisie, is something wrong?"

Nothing was wrong. Nothing was going on. Life continued much the same as it had for the past twenty years. He spent time with his daughter when he had it. Not as much as he should have. Way less than he should have, in fact. Hell, he was a fuck-up as a father. But for some reason his daughter loved him and he was eternally grateful for that.

She'd even forgiven him for never telling her the truth about her mother, that she was half *silvani*, one of the *Fata*, the Etruscan fairy races. She'd had to find out that one on her own.

Hell, life should be good.

So why did he feel so fucking restless?

"Hey, man, I don't wanna pry." Aule leaned forward. "You don't wanna talk to me, I'm good with that. But you—"

"I'm bored. It's stupid and childish and I feel like a fucking idiot admitting it but…" He sighed and took a deep pull on the beer. "I'm bored and…burned out."

Aule paused. "Then take a break. It's not like you haven't earned it."

Snorting, Kaisie shook his head. "What the hell would I do?"

"Take a vacation. Go to a casino, play some real table games. Ask a woman on a date."

"A date, huh?"

Aule's mouth curved in a grin. "Yeah. You remember those, right? You take a woman to dinner, maybe a movie before you ask her to sleep with you. You know, court her."

"Court?" Kaisie actually smiled. "When did you become such a fucking gentleman?"

"My mate would tell you I'm not, usually. But then she puts up with me day in and day out."

Kaisie nodded, but that ache in his chest had returned. The one he'd had earlier today. The one he didn't understand. And probably didn't want to know what caused it.

Since Aule continued to stare at him, Kaisie forced a smile, which his friend probably knew was fake. He didn't care. "Make my excuses, will ya? I think I'm gonna head out."

After a brief pause, Aule nodded. "Sure. Hey, stop for dinner. Mary'll make you ravioli. She knows you love it. Bring Kaine and John."

Grabbing his coat from the pile on the kitchen table, he left after telling Aule he'd call to set a date. Maybe he actually would this time.

Then again, he'd become so fucking antisocial lately, he probably wouldn't.

Stepping out of the house, he took a moment to just breathe in the cold air. February in Pennsylvania usually meant snow on the ground but the last snowfall had been in early December so the ground was frozen but not covered.

He thought about changing into his pelt and going for a run, maybe heading over to the Howling Wolf bar to listen to the Lady of the Silver Light, the Etruscan Moon Goddess Lusna, sing some blues.

He decided against it when he realized she'd probably want to talk to him and he had no desire to talk to anyone. Not even the *lucani*'s patron goddess.

He really was an antisocial son of a bitch.

Except, there was one person he would have no problem talking to right now.

And his feet had automatically pointed him in her direction.

He tried to ignore the impulse, tried to tell himself he was only walking back through the den, when his house was in the completely opposite direction, because he needed the exercise.

Shit. The least he could do was not lie to himself. He'd done enough of that through the years.

Soundlessly, he made his way through the wooded areas between the houses on the outskirts of the small *lucani* village and the more densely populated area closer to the community area.

The little house that was his target rested dead center in the village.

It only had five rooms and one floor but apparently she liked it. At least, she hadn't complained when Kyle had told her she'd be moving out of the holding facility where she'd been kept for months.

Kyle had figured she'd be safer surrounded on all sides than stuck on the outskirts of the village where he'd have to assign guards at all hours.

Besides, she wasn't going anywhere without her son. She'd made that perfectly clear.

No one had any reason to doubt her word not to leave the safety of that house after dark without an escort.

Kaisie figured she was tucked up tight inside. Probably not sleeping. Grace didn't look as if she got near enough sleep lately. Couldn't blame her for that.

If his child had been abducted by the *Mal*, he'd be going crazy with worry.

Grace seemed to be holding it together fairly well, actually.

Which was part of the reason he goaded her. When they verbally sparred, she didn't look as terrified.

Why that bothered him… Hell, he didn't have a fucking clue.

He reached the house in minutes then found himself leaning against an old pine at the back, where a large window looked straight through the tiny kitchen into the front room.

He knew she wasn't sleeping because he saw her, huddled on the couch, a mug in her hands as she stared at the TV, though he was pretty sure she wasn't watching the program.

He didn't take Grace for a fan of late-night infomercials about men's hair loss but he didn't really know Grace that well.

And right there was another problem.

He wanted to get to know her. He wanted to know about the shadows in her eyes and how she'd gotten that scar on her back. The one that looked like a burn.

He wanted to know what she liked to eat and what side of the bed she slept on. He wanted her to tell him who he could kill for putting that pain in her eyes and he wanted her to tell him she was never going back to the *Mal.*

Idiot.

Hell, he'd never wanted to kill for a woman before. He was a tracker. He wasn't *sicari,* an assassin.

But…he would kill for her.

He took a deep breath, barely scenting the two *lucani* out on patrol. Another *lucani* might not have been able to detect them. His powers of smell were just that much better.

Which meant he could smell her tears. With her face turned away from him, toward the TV, he couldn't see her crying but he knew she was.

Gods damn. Just… He sighed. Nortia, the Etruscan Goddess of Fate, must really have it in for him. What the hell had he done to piss her off?

He should go home. He needed to sleep. He hadn't had nearly enough to make up for the hours he'd missed when he was looking for her boy. And yeah, he was exhausted.

Besides, she wouldn't want him here. He'd frighten her if he knocked on the door this late at night.

But like every house in this village, there was a swinging door on the back entrance, just the right size for a large wolf to enter.

Even though the temperature hovered below freezing, he stripped down to his skin then folded his clothes and left them on the bench by the back door before he shifted.

Standing with his feet on the frozen ground, he called his wolf with little effort. The pain lasted only a few brief seconds. It ripped through him with the force of a bullet, tearing at his muscles and reshaping his bones before he stood on four paws and gave a full-body shake, just to make sure everything was where it was supposed to be.

It always was but he still checked every time. Force of habit.

Walking up to the back door, he found the latch to unlock the gate, easily manipulated by a wolf's paw, then slipped through into the kitchen.

As the panel swung shut with the barest hint of sound, he heard Grace gasp as she turned. Her gaze locked onto him immediately and he saw her scramble off the couch, nearly dropping the mug in her hand before she steadied it with her other.

He thought about shifting back, showing her who he was but when her eyes narrowed and her teeth bit into her bottom lip, he realized she knew it was him.

Then she confirmed it. "It's a little late for visiting, isn't it, Kaisie?"

Now there was the tone he wanted to hear in her voice, even if it was overlaid with the wet sound of the tears she'd been crying. That haughty, high-society drawl she used on him all the time. Nobody else, just him.

That tone did things to him…

He shook his head and walked around the couch, knowing she watched his every move. He didn't smell fear on her. If he had, he would have shifted back into his skin and gotten his clothes.

But he wanted to stay in his pelt. He wanted…

Jumping up onto the couch, he lay on his stomach, paws out in front of him, staring up at Grace.

She watched his every move with narrowed eyes but her teeth worried her lip until he thought she might break the skin.

With a huff, she pushed that gorgeous red hair over her shoulder and sat back down on the opposite end of the couch, a sectional with a chaise. She stretched her legs along the chaise but she didn't look at all comfortable.

"I don't know what you're doing here but I don't want to fight with you. Not now."

He didn't want to fight either. And he didn't want the entire width of a cushion to separate them.

Careful not to rip the fabric with his nails, he shimmied over onto that center cushion and pushed his snout against her leg.

She wore flannel pants that smelled like her. So damn soft against his nose. On top, a huge, old sweatshirt covered her from neck to thighs, faded and washed so many times, it felt like a baby's blanket. That smelled like her too.

Hot, sweet woman.

He squashed the growl building in his throat. She probably wouldn't understand that it wasn't an angry sound.

Nudging her leg again, he heard her huff. "You're pushy no matter what form you're in, aren't you? Do you want the entire couch?"

He shook his head then licked her nearest hand, clenched into a fist on her knee, and felt her shiver.

Her fingers straightened and flexed and she lifted her hand.

That was the opening he'd wanted. He laid his head where her hand had been, twisting his body onto his side and stretching out along the cushions.

For a full ten seconds, her hand hovered in the air over his body. He almost thought she was going to push him away.

Then her hand descended and her fingers settled onto his fur, gently, as if she were afraid she'd hurt him.

Or maybe she was afraid he'd snap at her.

He lay as still as possible, not wanting to spook her and after a few minutes, she started to run her hand along his fur.

No one but his daughter had ever petted him before. The sensation was strange. Nice but strange. Especially considering the feelings this woman riled in him.

Instead of the usual tension, his muscles relaxed and he huffed out a breath, which made her pause for a few seconds before she continued. They sat there in silence, the low drone from the television the only sound and the soft flicker of the screen the only light.

If he hadn't been so acutely aware of where he was and with whom, he might have fallen asleep. As it was, he had no problem staying awake so he could enjoy the sensation of her hand stroking through his thick fur.

Tinia's teat, if he'd known how fucking good this felt…

No, probably best not to go there. Because if he did, he might have to consider why he allowed her, of all people, to get this close.

After several minutes, he heard her sigh. "I keep wondering what he's doing. Does he think I've abandoned him? What lies has Ettore been telling him? Does someone read him a story before bed? Do they tuck him in? Is he feeling better or is he still sick?"

Kaisie heard the agony in her voice, the fear. It hit him in another part of his body, dead center in his chest.

"I don't know even know why Ettore took him. What's changed? Alex wasn't born *Mal,* not like—" She stopped to draw in a breath. "He didn't want him when he was born. Why would he change his mind now?"

Since Kaisie had no answers for her, he remained quiet, sensing she just needed to vent. She continued to pet him with a light touch even though her tone had hardened.

"I'm not a violent person. I've made horrible mistakes. The men I hired when I first started to look for the right donor for Alex's serum were animals. But I was desperate. I didn't know they'd murdered my test subjects. I should have. I make no excuses. But my son was dying. I'd already lost my daughter and I couldn't lose Alex."

At the mention of her daughter, he turned his head to look at her.

Tears welled in her eyes, which he could barely see because she refused to look down at him. He heard a soul-deep pain in her voice that called to the man. Again, he felt the urge to shift and take her into his arms.

He wondered if she'd let him.

Probably not.

Probably safer to stay in his pelt.

Shit. When had he become such a fucking pussy?

Then again, discretion really was the better part of valor occasionally.

And sometimes the feel of a woman's hand on your pelt was enough to make you stupid.

Chapter Two

For hours, Grace had been battling nausea, dizziness, muscle pain and a monstrous headache that she couldn't afford to turn into a migraine.

She didn't have to guess at the cause but she couldn't force herself to stop obsessing and get some sleep.

She needed to be sharp tomorrow, needed to prove herself worthy of her son. To be useful when the *lucani* went to rescue Alex.

But she couldn't sleep because she'd worked herself into a state of complete panic.

Until that damn wolf had walked through the doggie door.

Then she'd actually felt her muscles begin to relax. All because she knew exactly who this wolf was.

Now with her hand stroking his pelt and his head on her lap, she felt her nausea ease and the dizziness disappear.

Because of him.

He couldn't take away the fear, though. That remained a cold lump in her stomach, a raw ache in her chest.

But having Kaisie lying on the couch next to her made everything else settle.

And that should've been a scary thought.

Too bad everything else in her life was even more terrifying.

"We have to succeed tomorrow," she said, knowing he understood her. "And if we don't, at least Alex has to know we tried. I can't let him believe I abandoned him to that monster."

Kaisie's wolf whined and shook his head.

Amazingly, she knew exactly what he couldn't say.

"Yes, he could think that. He's only a boy. Whose mother has done awful things. Horrible..."

She'd done them to save her son, yes, but the blood of two young Etruscans was on her hands. The men she'd hired to kidnap her test subjects had been less than honorable.

"I know I should've known when I hired them. But Alex was dying. And I was naïve enough to think those men would simply release those young people. I didn't know they were going to kill them. I should have. I know I should have."

It was why she'd expected the *lucani* to simply kill her and be done with it.

She'd begged the *lucani* king, Colerus Luporeale, to promise her Alex would be well cared for, should anything happen to her.

He'd agreed without hesitation.

Which was why she was fully prepared to die tomorrow to ensure that Alex got out with the *lucani*. They wouldn't care if she didn't— Well, that wasn't completely true.

For some reason, the women here had rallied to her side. Probably only because she was Alex's mother. But they wouldn't miss her.

She'd also spoken to Tamra privately and coerced a promise from her. Alex would have another woman in his life to mother him if she didn't come back. Yes, he would miss her but eventually...

She sighed and Kaisie whined again, drawing her gaze back down to him.

In the darkness broken only by the soft glow from the television, she stared into the wolf's completely human eyes, so green they reminded her of spring grass.

Such beautiful eyes.

She'd harbored a *hopefully* well-guarded secret since she'd met Kaisie, one she really hoped no one ever discovered.

She thought he was wonderful. Sure, his manners could use a little polish and his hair needed a trim. And he definitely needed to shave that scruff off his face.

But the man was strong, fiercely loyal, smart as all hell and steady as a rock. Everything she'd always thought she wanted in a man.

She waited anxiously for the minute he walked through her door every day, longed to hear his deep voice, even though all they did was argue.

Oh, she realized he felt a faint spark of attraction for her. She wasn't an ugly cow with warts who weighed three hundred pounds.

She knew men usually were attracted by the red hair and the haughty looks. But the only men she'd known growing up had been introduced to her by her *Mal* grandmother or her *Mal*-brainwashed parents. Men who cared only for wealth and power and what she could mean to their careers.

They didn't care that she was a damn good scientist, that her dream date would be dinner and a show or that she loved to read to her son.

But she and Kaisie would never get beyond attraction. At least, *he* would never. She'd already lost half her heart.

And she wished he'd shift back into his skin so she could tell him to take her to bed. To take her mind off what was going to come tomorrow.

She'd never had sex just for pleasure. Sex had always been a duty, a chore. Sometimes it hadn't been consensual, though she'd never said no. If she'd ever said no…

She'd be like her older cousin Marie, spending her days staring out the window of her apartment in Manhattan, her mind a vast field of nothing, wiped clean by a spell to make her docile.

Marie was the perfect breeder. She'd already produced three *Mal* for the man her parents had sold her to.

Grace did not want to become Marie.

"Kaisie..."

She wanted him in his skin. She wanted him to take her to bed. To treat her like a woman instead of an object. She wanted, at least for tonight, to have sex that didn't leave her sobbing silently in the shower afterward.

But she couldn't ask. If he turned her down, she might not recover. She really didn't know why he was here.

She sighed. "I guess I should try to get some sleep. And so should you. I'm better now. Thank you. You don't have to stay any longer."

He growled, the sound low and deep but not scary. He was arguing with her.

Familiar ground.

"Don't dare start with me, Kaisie. I just...don't want to fight."

With a huff, the wolf scrambled off the couch and stood in front of her. She expected him to leave then. Instead, he started to change.

It only took seconds for the wolf to become a gorgeous man. A flash of brilliant color. A smudging of reality and then there he stood.

Beautiful. He was absolutely beautiful. The man was forty-four years old and he had the body of a man twenty years younger.

She let her gaze linger on his chest for several seconds. Broad, well muscled and lightly covered with dark hair, the skin darker than her own. Her lips parted to draw in breath and she tried not to sigh.

Instead she lifted her gaze to his face.

Her eyes widened.

He'd shaved. No, he'd trimmed. He'd cut off the scruff but still had dark stubble covering his chin and upper lip. She couldn't believe he'd left it as an affectation. He probably just hadn't wanted to take the time to shave completely.

Oh my Blessed Goddess, she'd never seen anything so sexy. It accentuated the rugged lines of his face and set off his wide green eyes.

He'd also cut his hair, not short, just long enough to show some wave.

Her stomach clenched with a hunger so fierce, she almost didn't recognize it for what it was.

She'd never wanted anyone before. Oh, maybe as a silly teenager, she'd imagined herself in lust with a boy from the exclusive prep school her parents had sent her to.

But at twenty, she'd learned just how cold sex could be. And she'd learned to submerge any hint of desire.

All those long-repressed longings roared up now with the fury of a hurricane.

Which didn't make any sense. She'd known this man less than a month.

And it didn't matter.

He didn't say anything as he reached for her, just wrapped both hands around her head and pulled her forward to meet his kiss.

She froze as his lips met hers, her eyes wide as his mouth moved over hers. Soft. Gentle. Enticing.

She hadn't known what to expect but it certainly hadn't been this melting warmth. His lips caressed hers, not forcing her mouth open but not static either. He kissed her, his lips in constant motion, roaming over hers, tasting her.

And she tasted him. Male heat and the faint bitterness of alcohol.

Maybe it was the alcohol making him want her.

Did it matter?

No. She needed him now.

Her lips began to soften and she tilted her head so she participated rather than just let it happen.

Her arms lifted and curved around his shoulders. The warmth of his body hit her like a blast furnace, seeping into her skin. Forcing unfamiliar emotion to simmer in her blood like lava.

With a tug on her hair, Kaisie tilted her head back even farther, his mouth leaving hers to bite and suck at her neck. Her skin stung wherever his lips landed and she knew she'd have bruises come daylight. She didn't care. They could be healed easily enough because they weren't deep. And maybe she'd let them stay because he'd given them to her in passion.

With her fingers clenched in his hair and her body pressed against his, she shut off her brain and gave herself over to the demands of mind-numbing sex.

And the feel of his swelling cock trapped between them.

Her arms tightened around him, as if afraid he'd try to get away. Which didn't seem very likely. His hands had slipped under her sweatshirt to spread across the bare skin of her back. She felt each of his fingers press against her and she wanted him to hold her harder. To lift the worn cotton over her head so he could put his mouth on her breasts.

She didn't know why she wanted that, had never wanted another man to do so. But her breasts ached and her nipples hardened into tight nubs that demanded his attention.

As if he'd read her mind, or maybe it was the way she rubbed against him, he cupped her breasts in his hands, kneading the mounds and taking her breath away.

She gasped, stilling as she tried to absorb the sensations he created.

"Do you like that?" He spoke against the hollow of her throat, his breath heating her skin. She shivered in reaction. "Yeah, I think you do. Hang tight, babe. It'll get better."

With a few deft movements, he stripped her top over her head, leaving her bare from the waist up.

Grace had a moment to panic as his gaze dropped. She'd had two children. Her breasts weren't as firm as they'd been years ago. And while she didn't consider herself fat, she did carry a few more pounds than she wanted.

Her skin was pale but littered with freckles, a defect her mother had agonized over when she was a child. She was marred. Imperfect.

Is that what Kaisie would see too?

Her breath caught in her throat as he continued to stare at her without speaking. His expression had gone taut and she couldn't tell if he found her lacking or—

"Tinia's teat, you're fucking beautiful." His hands molded to her breasts again, his thumb and forefinger pinching the nipples until she thought she might implode.

Or come. Something else she'd never experienced from a hand other than her own.

Her knees threatened to buckle but she locked them, her hands settling back on his shoulders to help her balance.

She wanted to speak, to tell him she felt the same way about him. That he made her weak-kneed and hot and wet between her thighs. But she could only stand there and watch him lower his head to wrap his lips around one nipple and suck it into his mouth.

Oh gods. Her knees did buckle then but Kaisie wrapped an arm around her waist and held her upright while he sucked and nipped at her breast.

Heat washed over her, electrifying her skin and making her sex throb. Her head fell back as he switched sides, thoroughly pleasuring that nipple as well.

She'd never imagined how good sex could be and this was only foreplay. If he stopped now, she didn't think she'd ever be able to pick up the pieces.

Clinging to him, she concentrated on the feel of his lips, the press of his muscled thighs against hers and the thick hardness of his cock brushing against her stomach.

Her hips shifted restlessly, trying to ease the ache between her thighs. She wanted him to lift her and impale her, take her hard and fast and leave her sated and breathless.

But Kaisie obviously had other ideas.

With a final lick, he pulled back and caught her gaze, those green eyes even brighter. "Tell me you want me. I need to hear you say it."

She swallowed at the harsh sound of his voice but her body responded with a shiver of pure lust. "I want you. On the floor, the couch, against the wall. I don't care. Just take me. Before I collapse."

He barely gave her time to breathe before he sealed his mouth over hers and kissed her until she started to float.

Which turned out to be Kaisie lifting her off her feet and swinging her into his arms. He had no trouble taking her weight, making her feel sexy and desirable with every kiss, every touch.

With their lips fused, he started to walk. She thought he'd go for the couch but he headed for the small bedroom at the back, where the queen-size mattress should be more than big enough to accommodate two people. At least, it'd seemed huge and empty to her this past week.

Now with Kaisie coming down on top of her, she barely even noticed the bed because all she could concentrate on was him.

He'd released her mouth again to let his lips travel. From her jaw to her neck and below. He stopped to tease her breasts again while his hands worked at her flannel pants. The pants had seen better days and she didn't care if he ripped them off, even if they were favorites. But he treated them as if they were expensive lingerie, easing them down her hips and pushing them to her feet where she finally kicked them off.

She hadn't been wearing underwear and the cooler air hit her overheated skin, causing goose bumps to rise.

Without saying a word, Kaisie rose to his knees, lifted her off the bed and pulled down the comforter and sheet to place her under them.

Sliding in after her, he surprised her with a smile, visible in the dim light from the bedside lamp she'd turned on earlier. Alex had trouble sleeping in the dark and she always left a nightlight on for him.

It was a habit she'd taken up herself. Did he have a nightlight now? Was—

"Hey, come back to me, Grace. You can't do anything right now except be here with me."

She refocused on his smile, forcing herself to return it. She knew hers probably looked unnatural and she couldn't hold it anyway. Not when he ran a hand down her body, stroking her like she'd stroked his pelt earlier.

And scattering her thoughts when he let his fingers brush over her clit.

Her eyes began to close as her hips arched into his hand, trying to get him to stroke her harder, to get her off and ease this ache.

"I need you to make me come."

"I will, sweetheart. Just not yet. Open your eyes and watch me."

His voice held a note of command she didn't care to disobey. She looked up then, followed his gaze to where his hand hovered over her mound. She kept her pubic hair trimmed close and her pussy lips bare. The skin there felt sensitive and swollen, throbbing in anticipation.

She drew in a deep breath then held it as his hand closed the short distance between them. His fingers slipped between her thighs and she let them fall open another few inches. She thought he'd hurry now but his fingers only grazed along her folds, setting off sizzling jolts of sensation that made her sex clench.

She moaned, the sound loud and slightly embarrassing in the quiet of the little house. But Kaisie's mouth curved in a masculine smile and he bent to nip at her breast then lower, on her hipbone as he let his fingers play along her slit.

Her hands twisted in the sheets, frustration and lust a heady combination. Her body felt lightning-struck, her nerve endings sizzling and popping under the skin. She almost forgot that she could touch him. She'd never been allowed to do what she wanted in bed before.

As if he'd read her mind, he whispered in her ear. "Touch me, Grace. I won't break."

She froze, unsure what he'd like. Should she reach for his cock, wrap her hand around it and stroke him? Or could she pet his body like she'd done with his wolf earlier?

"Grace, don't think. Just do it."

His voice had hardened, whether with lust or impatience, she didn't know. So she lifted one hand and put it on his chest. She stroked her fingers through the crisp hair as she would his pelt. And felt his chest expand as he drew in a deep breath.

"That's right. Put your hands on me."

Her other hand rose and joined the first then she lost herself in the pleasure of touching him.

His fingers stilled, resting on her thigh while she began her exploration of him. First, she stroked across his shoulders, warm skin stretched over strong bone, then down his arms, muscles taut.

Back to his chest where she let her fingers pluck at his nipples, her gaze darting back to his when he sucked in a sharp breath.

"Harder."

The word escaped between his gritted teeth, making a smile curve her own lips. He liked it when she rolled the pointed nubs between her fingers. It showed in the way his eyelids fell and his head tilted back. With more confidence, she scraped her nails down his stomach to the mat of dark curls at the base of his cock.

She carefully avoided making contact with his shaft, afraid to touch him there without an explicit command. She didn't want to hurt him or displease him in any way. In her experience, men wanted what they wanted when they wanted it and only how they wanted it. What she'd wanted had never mattered.

"Do you… Should I…"

She didn't know what he wanted and every insecurity she'd ever had about sex now raised its ugly head.

Her chest began to ache and she felt out of breath. She took a deep breath but couldn't seem to get enough air. She knew she was starting to hyperventilate, knew she needed to calm down but couldn't seem to stop.

Tears welled in her eyes as she watched Kaisie's eyes narrow. Blessed Goddess, why was he here? What did he see in her that had brought him to her bed?

Was she just a willing body? Someone he knew wouldn't say no? Did he—

His fingers began to stroke her and her body responded with a fresh surge of lust, sweeping her fears away in a heated rush. Moisture slicked her lower lips, her sheath tightened, begging to be filled.

"Kaisie."

"That's right, sweetheart." He coated his fingers in her moisture, his thumb pressing against her clit with steady pressure. "I'm right here. Nobody else. Just me."

He slipped one finger between her folds and into her tight channel. She hissed at the invasion and her hands reached for his shoulders again as her body buzzed.

"No, don't take your hand away. Wrap your hand around my cock, baby. I want you to stroke me."

She latched on to his raspy demands like a lifeline and lowered one hand to follow his command.

Goddess, he was hot. Hard, silky, burning hot. And thick. Beautiful.

She wrapped one hand around him and he groaned, low and deep as she started to stroke him. Tentatively at first then with more surety as he responded to her touch.

He lowered his head to kiss her again, his tongue slipping between her lips to tangle with hers as his fingers slipped into her body.

Her body went liquid as her hand tightened around him. His cock swelled, throbbing in her hand and she stroked him faster. She wanted him closer, wanted him to take her.

She was ready. Gods, she didn't think she could be any more ready. She'd pushed all the other stuff away as his thumb pressed against her clit, tormenting the little nub while he slipped a second finger into her sheath and began to fuck her with them.

"That's it, *kareta*. Fuck, the look on your face…"

She had no idea what she looked like and didn't care as long as he continued to make her feel like this. Fizzy and tight and on the edge of something wonderful.

A haze of pleasure settled over her. Even though she hadn't found her release yet, she could be content with just this feeling of tension. With his fingers gliding inside her.

But Kaisie wouldn't be content. She had to make him come, had to satisfy him.

With one hand on his shoulder and the other wrapped around his cock, she tried to urge him closer. Instead, he leaned back, his hand slipping from between her legs.

She took a breath, getting ready to protest but he startled her by falling onto his back then motioning for her to—what?

"Come here, Grace. On top."

She blinked. She'd never done it this way. "I don't—"

"On your knees, *kareta*, then straddle my hips. Trust me. Come here."

He smiled at her—grinned, actually. And her heart stuttered at the beauty of it. At the ease and the grace of it.

Blessed Goddess, she wanted to be worthy of it.

His smile never faltered as he either didn't notice or conveniently ignored her hesitation. And it turned downright sinful when she got to her knees and did as he'd told her.

Straddling his thighs, she awkwardly moved into the position he wanted her. She understood the basic concept but this position left her completely exposed, naked with her legs spread. Yes, she was on top but—

"Grace, honey, come up here. Closer."

That voice wiped away her fears with its husky growl and, when he put his hands on her hips to help her along, she nearly melted from the heat.

"Just a little farther… Now take me, babe."

She swallowed as he took her hand and guided it once again to his cock. "Pull me back, kinda like putting a car in gear."

Her lips curved in a smile and laughter bubbled in her chest even as her legs quaked with lust. He was so hard, she had to use a little force to align him with her entrance.

But when she did, she groaned as the silky, fat tip slid through her folds.

"Fuck, woman, you're so fucking hot. Come on, babe. Take me."

With one hand braced in his, she used the other to hold him straight before she began to lower onto him.

The thick tip lodged at the entrance to her sex and she shuddered at the intimacy of the sensation. Her gaze locked with his, her hand tightening on his until she was sure she'd leave bruises. He didn't seem to mind, just held her steady as she let gravity work to take him into her body.

He felt enormous, splitting her open, filling her with heat and making her skin feel too tight for her body.

For a brief second, she thought she wouldn't be able to take all of him and she froze. The pleasure scared her, the overwhelming sense that she was losing control of herself.

She fought against it, even as she knew it was a losing battle. Kaisie wasn't going to let her retain any semblance of control.

He lifted his hips to close those few remaining centimeters and she drew in a deep breath as overpowering emotion swept through her. She couldn't get enough air, couldn't move or think. Couldn't do anything but feel.

And that was one subject where she had no experience.

She wanted to experience the high of a great release without an emotional attachment.

But as much as she'd tried not to build any relationships, this man had blown through her defenses and carved a space for himself in her heart.

With that realization, her body tightened around him, making his eyes narrow and forcing a groan from deep in his throat.

"Grace." His voice made her swallow convulsively. "Move."

She obeyed without thought, lifting her body in breath-stealing increments. Her sheath clung to his cock, reluctant to release him. The tension built as she rose and continued to increase when she sank back down.

Her eyes closed as they found a rhythm that sent sharp bolts of pleasure spearing between her thighs. He moved with her, easing back as she lifted up then sliding home, faster each second.

Her other hand reached out, seeking an anchor and Kaisie's was there to grab it, to twine their fingers together and hold her upright as her body began to quiver.

"There, Gracie. That's— *Fuck.*"

She opened her eyes and saw that his were closed, his features taut with lust. She knew the expression well.

But then he opened his eyes and she realized she'd never seen that depth of emotion on any man's face.

She came without warning, like a lightning strike that lit her up from the inside out. Her sheath gripped him like a fist as sensation shot from her womb up her back to her brain.

With a cry, she arched her back, her hips grinding down on his, trying to prolong the sensation that threatened her sanity. Her pussy milked him until his hips slammed into hers and she felt his cock twitch and spill heat inside her.

Unable to hold herself upright, she sagged and fell against his chest. She didn't fall far. He lifted his upper body off the bed to meet her.

Her overheated skin met his burning-hot flesh and she melted into him, her lungs gasping for air, tears welling in her eyes.

His breath warmed her cheek as he panted, clearly as out of breath as she was.

She liked that. A lot.

She wanted to wrap him in her arms but she couldn't get them to move. Exhaustion hit her like a sledgehammer and she couldn't keep her eyes open.

"It's okay, Grace." His voice sank into her head and lulled her into a sense of security she couldn't fight. "Go ahead. Sleep. I'm not leaving."

She didn't remember anything after that.

Chapter Three

Kaisie woke just before the sun rose, like he always did, even though he'd only gotten a few hours of sleep.

It was a few hours more than he'd had in the past couple of weeks and he'd woken feeling completely rested.

The fact that he'd practically fucked the woman in his arms into unconsciousness last night made his jaw lock but he'd be damned if he'd second-guess it now.

She'd needed the rest and he knew she wouldn't have slept without a distraction.

He just hadn't counted on her being one hell of a distraction for him.

And he couldn't afford any distractions today. Not if he wanted to keep her alive.

He let his gaze trace her sharp features, relaxed now in sleep. He'd have to wake her soon. Kyle planned to leave at eight a.m. for the Reading airport, where they'd chartered a plane to Florida for the group storming Marrucini's compound. They had an alternate means of egress. Actually, they had two but this woman didn't know that.

She hadn't asked. She'd only made Cole promise that the team would get Alex out.

With a soft sigh, she turned, her face pressing into his chest, eyes still closed. His arms tightened, pulling her even closer, as he willed his body to behave. They didn't have time for anything more than showers and breakfast. He planned to make sure she ate. She'd probably fight him about it. She fought him about everything, which, he had to say, he kinda liked.

Fucked up? Yeah. He didn't care.

He knew he should get up, get in the shower and start breakfast. And bring his clothes in off the porch. They'd be ice cold and need to thaw before he put them on.

Screw it.

He lowered his head and buried his nose in her hair. She smelled amazing. Spicy and sweet and *his*.

And he really needed to feed her before they went to take back her son.

Pressing a kiss to the top of her head, he eased out of bed, making sure she was covered so she didn't get cold.

After a quick shower, he raided the small fridge and started cooking.

She woke just as he was about to set the scrambled eggs and bacon on the breakfast bar. She literally hadn't had anything else in the house, which pissed him off.

What the hell had she been eating?

Apparently not much.

He didn't turn when he heard her stop in the doorway between the bedroom and the rest of the house. He just went back to the kitchen, which was nothing more than a row of appliances separated from the rest of the living area by the bar.

After he'd poured orange juice—the milk had gone stale and he'd tossed it—he set that on the bar as well. Then he looked at her.

She hadn't moved, her eyes wide and her teeth worrying the hell out of her bottom lip. She'd already dressed in the clothes he'd asked Kaine to drop off yesterday.

She looked nervous but no longer exhausted. At least the dark circles were gone from beneath her eyes.

She waved a shaking hand at herself. "I assumed I was supposed to put these on."

"You assumed right. Come on and eat. We'll be leaving soon."

"You shouldn't have bothered. I don't think I can stomach anything."

"You can and you will. You can't function on an empty stomach."

A brief flash of rebellion sparked in her eyes but her stomach growled loudly enough that she blushed. Still, she didn't give in right away and he hid a smile. Glad to know she still had that backbone he admired so damn much.

"Maybe just a little."

He just nodded.

She dropped his gaze and walked to the bar as he sat. There were only two chairs so she had to sit next to him.

"Did you make coffee by any chance?"

"Didn't find any in the cupboards, sorry." A small lie. He hadn't come across coffee until he'd glanced in the freezer for food but she didn't need a stimulant to make her more jumpy today.

She eyed the glass with a wry twist to her lips. "I'd rather have milk. I get the juice for Alex."

Which proved his theory that she hadn't been eating. "The milk went bad a few days ago. Drink the juice."

She stiffened and flashed him a quick glare, even as she picked up her fork. "I'm not a child."

He grinned at her, letting a little of the heat from last night enter his gaze. "I know that. Firsthand."

She sucked in a short, sharp breath and her pale skin flushed bright red. Her mouth opened then closed as she thought better of a response. Or maybe she just couldn't think of one.

Then she picked up her fork and they spent the next few minutes eating in silence.

When she'd finished almost everything, she sighed before taking her plate to the dishwasher.

He watched as she squared her shoulders before turning back around to face him. "I want you to promise me something."

He'd been waiting for this. "Tell me what it is and I'll let you know if I can."

"Promise me you'll make sure Alex gets out no matter what."

He nodded. "I promise to do everything I can to make that happen."

Her eyes dipped and her teeth came out to nibble on her bottom lip. "Thank you. And…I have another request."

His eyebrows lifted as he waited, having no idea what she was about to ask.

"If my daughter's there… I—I want you to help me get her out."

He'd heard about the daughter from Dr. Dane Dimitriou, heard about the circumstances of her birth. And he could see the anguish even now in Grace's eyes. He'd kill Marrucini with his bare hands if he had the chance.

But… "Will she know who you are? Will she leave with you willingly?"

He felt like the world's biggest son of a bitch when tears welled in her eyes again but she held his gaze. "No, I don't think she'll know me. And I don't think she'll go willingly. I just…need to try. She's only fifteen, Kaisie. If we get lucky, she won't have come into her full power yet. It usually hits at puberty. I didn't hit puberty until I was sixteen and then my power was mostly harmless. I'm hoping…maybe…"

That maybe the girl who'd been born *Mal* and reared by the ruthless bastard who was her father hadn't turned completely evil. That she could be saved.

But as far as Kaisie knew, no one had ever escaped the *Mal*'s hold. And how could they? They were literally *born* evil, cursed to crave power and wealth and lacking any instinct for good.

"I can't promise that, Grace. If it comes down to Alex or the girl, we take Alex. But if we get an opportunity, I'll try."

She forced a smile. "That's all I ask. Thank you."

* * * * *

The flight to Florida was shorter than she'd expected and surprisingly quiet, considering there were ten people in the airplane.

Grace knew most of them. Kaisie, of course, sitting next to her, his eyes closed. His daughter Kaine and her mate John in the row next to them.

Kyle, Duke and Nic, Kaine's fellow *sicarii*, sat in the two rows beyond Kaine. Another two *lucani*, Seth and Race, sat near the front of the cabin, along with another man Grace had never met. He gave off a steady wave of power that she couldn't mistake. Or decipher.

She figured he was a *stregone*, a male witch, though they typically didn't have that much power. But this one…

Sighing, she shook her head. She should try to get some rest but she couldn't get her brain to shut off.

Last night…

She didn't regret a single minute. She only wished—

No. No wishing. She needed to stay focused on the task ahead.

She couldn't let herself consider failure. They would get Alex back.

They had to. Alex would be waiting for them, praying for her to come get him.

And her daughter…

If her daughter was there, she wasn't leaving without her.

"Grace."

Kaisie's voice startled her out of her thoughts and her gaze snapped to his. Her breath caught in her throat at the intensity in his eyes and the attraction she felt whenever she looked at him hit her low in her body, right between her legs.

Damn him. Last night had been amazing. At least for her. She'd almost expected him to be gone this morning when she woke. And to ignore her today as if nothing had happened between them.

But now he acted as if he actually cared about what happened to her. As if he didn't care who knew.

He was confusing the almighty hell out of her so she kept her mouth shut and waited for him to continue.

"You have the knife?"

He'd given her a blade in a plain leather sheath she now had strapped around her waist. "You helped me strap it on."

His gaze narrowed. "Don't take it off."

She nodded though she knew she'd take it off in a heartbeat. If it came down to her son and daughter or the knife, she'd give up the knife. Knowing that it might cost her her life.

Kaisie kept staring at her, as if he knew exactly what she was thinking, as if he wanted her to confess.

But one night of great sex did not give him the right to tell her what to do.

So she just stared back.

But she couldn't hold his gaze.

She heard him sigh as she turned to look out the window, where the ground was fast approaching. The plane had begun its descent and they'd be landing in minutes. It wouldn't take long to get to the compound and they were counting on the element of surprise to get them in and out with a minimum of bloodshed.

For the next few minutes, she tried to clear her mind of everything but her goal—get her kids. Even the one who might not want her.

* * * * *

"Kaine."

"What's up, Dad?"

Kaisie drew his daughter around to the far side of the idling plane, where no one would hear them over the noise from the engines.

"Whatever happens, you don't leave her side."

Kaine didn't look surprised by his demand, just waited for him to continue.

"I think she's gonna do something stupid."

Kaine's head cocked to the side. "Like?"

Like trade herself for Alex. Or do something even more stupid and get herself killed in pursuit of her daughter.

Even though Kaisie knew he'd do the same thing for his own daughter.

"Just stick with her. Let the others get the kid."

"Okay."

Her easy acceptance made him smile.

But it died a quick death as the group got into the two vans they'd had waiting for them at the private airport only twenty minutes from Marrucini's compound on the outskirts of Tampa.

Since everyone knew the plan, there wasn't a lot of talk during the drive and they drove to the staging area in relative silence.

He watched Grace without trying to make it obvious that he was watching her, while she kept her gaze carefully trained out the front window. He saw her skin pale with each mile marker, her eyelids flutter when they turned off Interstate 4 to wind through an industrial area to get to their destination.

Race had somehow found an abandoned warehouse near the border of Marrucini's property where they could park the vans and change, for those shifting into their pelts.

Kaisie could see the silence was starting to get to Grace so before he shifted, he asked John to keep her company until they were ready to head out.

By the time he dropped his black-leather collar by his side, removed his clothes and put them in the backpack John would carry, he felt ready to crawl out of his skin. Because she looked ready to do the same.

Chill, old man. You won't be able to function if you don't chill.

Through sheer force of will, he pushed the doubts to the back of his mind and called his wolf.

When he stood on four paws instead of two feet, he shook his head and his tail then picked up his leash and trotted over to Grace, where he dropped it at her feet.

He didn't know if she realized what he was offering her at that moment. John did, though, which was why he didn't bend to pick up the collar.

Grace stared at it for a second before she looked at John, questions in her eyes.

"He wants you to put it on for him."

After a moment's hesitation, she knelt down, picked up the collar and took a few seconds to examine how it worked. She ran her fingers over the embedded tracker and the latch designed to break apart with the right motion.

Then she looked at him. And he knew she'd figured out what he was offering her.

She bit her lip before she got onto her knees in front of him and fastened the collar with gentle fingers.

Each collar was specially made for the wearer and fit perfectly. So she didn't need to fuss with it or let her fingers smooth his fur around the leather. He let her do it, actually tipped his head to the side so she could scratch his neck for a few stolen seconds before she stood.

"All right, people." Kyle waited by the door, his dark gaze taking in everything. "In and out. Fast and clean. Let's go."

Kaisie asked the Blessed Mother Goddess to give them a fucking break and headed for the door on Grace's heels.

* * * * *

Grace had assumed it would come down to a scene much like this.

She just hadn't imagined it would happen so easily.

She and the *lucani* had infiltrated Marrucini's compound with a minimum of drama. No flashing lights, no screaming alarms.

They'd snuck onto the property at different entry points, the stranger who'd joined them on the plane working a complicated spell that had weakened both the magical wards surrounding the grounds and the sophisticated alarm system that served as its backup.

She had no time to wonder who the man was because they were moving.

The wolves had streaked across the expanse of needle-sharp green blades that passed for grass in Florida, racing for their point of entry.

The rest of them on two legs had followed as quickly as they could.

She went as fast as she could, yet still lagged behind everyone except John, Kaine's mate, who stuck to her side like glue.

By the time they reached the house, Kyle, now in his skin and dressed, had opened the door that had led them into a mudroom that backed into the kitchen.

Since it was the middle of the night, the two rooms were empty, as was the hallway outside the kitchen.

She'd thought, *This is just too easy*, right before a guard passed the outside door they'd just entered.

Holding her breath until he'd continued on, after checking to see that the door was locked, she'd tried not to make too much noise as she replaced much-needed air in her lungs.

John had touched her shoulder, his expression concerned, but she'd shook her head just once and waited for Kyle to give them the go-ahead.

She, John and Kaine had been assigned to check the first floor, probably because Kyle knew most of the action would probably take place upstairs in the bedrooms. And he didn't want her in the way.

She could live with that, as long as Kaisie kept his promise and found her daughter.

No one had expected Ettore to walk into the kitchen.

Grace froze at the sight of the man who still managed to give her nightmares after all these years. Ettore looked like any other middle-aged man in baggy jeans and a loose t-shirt.

But this man was a monster.

Her heart tripped all over itself as her fight-or-flight mechanism kicked in.

But she didn't have time to pick one because John shoved her behind him, so hard she cried out as she hit the floor.

Her cry was lost in Kaine's snarl as she leaped for Ettore, aiming for his throat.

Which he countered by disappearing.

With nothing to stop her forward momentum, Kaine sailed into the double ovens on the wall then fell to the ground with a painful-sounding yip that had John rushing to her side.

Leaving Grace to scramble to her feet by herself. She got about halfway up when pain shot through her scalp as someone grabbed her hair.

Ice coated her veins at his touch. She knew it was him. He'd held her this way too many times for her to scrub the memory from her brain.

And when she felt the prick of a blade at her throat, she prayed that Kaisie would remember his promise.

Because she was about to pay for her transgressions.

* * * * *

Kaisie, now in his skin, and Race, his claws silent on the wood floor, climbed the back staircase to the third floor where they were pretty sure the boy was being held.

They hadn't encountered any security of any kind, either magical or electronic and Kaisie couldn't decide if it was hidden so well, they'd missed it, or if Marrucini was that damn sure of his wards and outdoor security.

Then he'd wondered if maybe the guy had known they were coming and was drawing them farther into the building before picking them off one by one.

They'd encountered no security men inside the house and Kaisie just couldn't wrap his head around that.

It made him that much more tense as they went deeper into the house.

"This guy's a fucking idiot or we're about to get out asses handed to us."

Race apparently agreed. At least that's what Kaisie assumed Race meant when he shook his head.

As they reached the top of the stairs, Kaisie finally detected the faint scent he was searching for.

The boy was up here. Somewhere.

And so was someone else. A female.

A nanny? Nurse? Or Grace's daughter?

Didn't matter. They'd sort that out later. First get the boy.

Signaling for Race to follow him, Kaisie started off across the sitting room that opened at the top of the stairs. Three doors stood on the opposite side of the room and Kaisie followed his nose to the one in the center.

The boy was through that door. But he wasn't alone.

He waited until he had Race's attention then held up two fingers. When Race nodded, Kaisie started a countdown with his fingers.

On one, he turned the handle and opened the door.

Kaisie heard nothing, no change in breathing, no movement. So he stuck his head through the door.

And caught sight of the gun leveled at his head.

"You don't want to come any closer."

The female voice was young but steady, as was the gun.

Kaisie froze, holding his hand behind his back in a fist to stop Race from showing himself.

He didn't want to spook the girl and have her blow a hole through him. She might not hit his head but who knew what she could hit.

Then he held out his hands in front of him, palms up. "We're not here to harm anyone. We're just here for the boy. He doesn't belong here."

"Well, you can't have him, so fuck off."

The obscenity, said in that little girl's voice, drew Kaisie's eyes away the gun and up to her face.

And his mouth dropped open.

The girl had dark hair but no one would mistake her for anyone but Grace's daughter.

She had the same dark eyes, the same slashing cheekbones.

And the same stubborn mouth.

Behind her on the bed, a boy peeked over her shoulder.

Kaisie directed his smile at him. "Alex? Hey. I'm Kaisie. I'm Kaine's dad."

The girl's mouth tightened even more. "You don't talk to him. And you need to leave. Just back out of the door and don't come back."

"Amy." Alex lowered his voice to a whisper but Kaisie heard him loud and clear. "I told you they'd come for me."

The girl's gaze never wavered from Kaisie's. "I'm not going to say it again. You need to leave."

Kaisie shook his head. "I'm not leaving without the boy. But you can come too. If you want."

Her eyes widened for a second before they narrowed back down. But in that brief moment, Kaisie saw something he recognized. Kaine had been a teenager not that long ago and he saw some of Kaine's strength in this girl.

"Alex, why don't you come on over here with me? We've gotta get going. Your mom's anxious to see you." He looked at the girl. "Both of you."

The gun shook. "I don't have a mother."

"Yeah, you do. She's downstairs waiting for us. But we need to go now."

"Who says I want to leave?"

"You told me you'd come with me." Alex's voice held a hint of tears and the girl dropped her gaze to look at him. "Please, I wanna go. Please come with me. I don't like it here."

Behind him, Race gave a barely audible whine and Alex's gaze shot toward the door, a grin curving his lips. "Is Kaine here?"

"Yes. And John. They're with your mom." Kaisie took a step forward, his gaze locked with the girl. "We're out of time. We've got to go." The girl tracked him with the gun as he stopped directly in front of her. "You coming?"

Her jaw quivered for a split second before she lowered the gun to her lap. It looked like an ink spot on the innocent white lace of her nightgown.

Then she slipped off the bed. "Let me get our backpacks."

He wanted to say no but girls needed their things. "Hurry."

Turning to sit on the bed, he patted his shoulder as the girl ran to the closet in the corner. "Jump on, Alex."

The boy threw his arms around Kaisie's neck and awkwardly wrapped his legs around his waist, as if his legs still weren't working properly. Kaisie knew the boy had been unable to walk before he'd been kidnapped. Something to worry about later.

The girl ran to the doorway then skidded to a stop, her eyes wide as she came face-to-face with Race's wolf.

"He won't hurt you. Just stick close to me…"

"Amalia," Alex whispered in his ear. "But she likes to be called Amy."

"Is he *lucani*?" Amy looked torn between wonder and fear.

"Yes. There are more around too, so don't be surprised if you see them. And don't shoot them."

She nodded, the gun in her hand pointed at the floor. He noticed she handled the weapon like someone who'd been doing it for years. "We need to leave before my—before anyone realizes what's going on. I hope you've got a damn good exit strategy."

Kaisie spared her a smile as Race took off for the stairs. "Don't worry, kid. We're professionals."

* * * * *

"I never expected to see you again, Grace." Ettore gave her hair a tug so hard, it forced tears into her eyes as the cold steel of a knife pressed against her throat. "I honestly never thought you'd have the courage to do something this…misguided."

Grace clamped her lips shut against the panicked cry that rose in her throat. She didn't want to give Ettore the satisfaction nor did she want to engage him in any kind of conversation. But if he was focused on her then everyone else could focus on getting out of the house. With her children.

"I guess I should be glad you haven't been pining away for me." She straightened, trying to ease his hold on her hair as she watched John take up a defensive position in front of Kaine, who hadn't moved.

If he'd hurt Kaisie's daughter…

"Don't think I haven't been keeping an eye on you, dear." His warm breath brushed against her hair, making her shiver. "The animals may have gotten their claws into you for a little while but you've returned to me now, haven't you?"

She'd kill herself before she allowed him to keep her here. But she'd make sure the wolves got out first.

And with the knife he held at her throat, it would be so easy to twist her head and—

"I didn't realize you'd gotten so lax in your old age, Ettore. Or is it simply your arrogance that's grown? Your security is abysmal. Obviously your standards have plummeted."

She cringed inwardly to hear her tone of voice. She didn't sound like herself. At least, not like the woman she'd become. The woman Kaisie had made love to last night.

No, she sounded like the creature this man had forced her to be from the age of twenty until he'd thankfully tossed her aside ten years ago.

He laughed, the sound sending shivers up her spine. She'd always thought his laugh revealed his evil heart. Others thought it was charming. She heard only the sneer and the arrogance.

"Oh, I think you'll be surprised how truly effective my security is. We may have allowed your little party to believe they'd entered unnoticed. But don't think you'll be leaving as easily."

"You're lying." Grace could sneer pretty damn well when she wanted to. She'd learned from him, after all. "Don't you think I learned anything from my so-called marriage to you? You're slipping."

This time, he gave a vicious yank and she couldn't help the short cry that escaped her lips.

"Well, well, it looks like you've grown a backbone since I threw you away. Too bad it won't do you any good now. I may have been too hasty about releasing you before but, trust me, I don't make the same mistake twice."

And she refused to live that way again. She'd die first.

"Now," he continued, "why don't you call your merry little band of invaders together before I decide you're not worth the effort and kill you before my security massacres your friends?"

He was bluffing. She'd known him long enough to recognize that tone in his voice. But about what? She couldn't make a mistake, couldn't risk the lives of her children or the *lucani*.

Ettore had power, much more than she did. And he'd perfected the use of it. He could move himself and others from one place to another, as he had when he'd kidnapped Cat, Evie and Alex. But he required a great deal of power and preparation. He needed to charge his magical batteries, so to speak, and usually he did that with sex.

Which made her realize he probably had another woman stashed away here. Possibly other children.

"It won't matter what you do to me." She had to keep him talking. Kaisie and the others had to have found the children by now. They had to be making their way out of the house. "The *lucani* don't care about me. Go ahead. Kill me. But don't imagine you can use me as a bargaining chip. Trust me, they won't hesitate to kill me to get to you."

* * * * *

Kaisie picked up the conversation from the kitchen as they reached the top of the stairs.

He stopped, holding up his fist to signal Race and Amy to halt. The girl froze as if she were doing an impression of a statue. Stone silent, as if she'd had practice making herself invisible.

The only response Alex made was to tighten his arms around Kaisie's neck. He, too, managed not to make more than the barest breath of sound.

But even with his enhanced hearing, Kaisie couldn't make out exactly what they were saying. He only knew he heard Grace and another man's voice. And Grace didn't sound like herself.

What the hell—

Race's snout nudged his knee just as Kaisie caught the scent of two men. Close and getting closer.

Behind them.

Son of a bitch.

Kaisie signaled Race to check out the threat coming up on their backs before he stepped into the stairwell. It'd been too easy to get in. It had to have been a trap.

But the only way out was to go down. Even if they went out a window, Alex would be a liability.

They encountered no one on the stairs, but Kaisie sensed more movement throughout the house now. As if someone had been lying in wait for them.

Shit, shit and double shit.

Where were Kaine and John? Were they hurt? What the hell was Grace saying?

He needed to get closer but he had to get the kids out first.

There had to be another way out.

"Amy."

The girl's pale, steady eyes met his.

"Exits. Second floor."

She nodded, pointed down and then to the left.

Kaisie looked up the stairs. No Race.

He couldn't wait for the other soldier. He had to get the kids to the *stregone* waiting outside to magically transport Alex and Amy back to the den. The *stregone* was strong enough to take both of them at once but it was a one-way trip.

Without the kids, though, Kaisie and the others wouldn't have to worry about them getting hurt.

He started down the stairs, knowing Amy would follow him. When he reached the second floor, he stuck his head out and saw nothing but an empty hall.

A tug on his shirt made him look back. Amy was shaking her head, her eyes now wide as she kept turning to look over her shoulder.

He got the hint. They needed to go now. She must have heard the muted sounds of a struggle on the floor above. Race had apparently found trouble.

The wolf would have to fend for himself for a few minutes.

Looking both ways down the hall, Alex's slight weight still firmly on his back, he reached for Amy's arm and drew her into his side. He felt her stiffen at the contact but she didn't push him away.

She led him halfway down the hall to a closed door that looked like all the others. Opening it, she pulled him inside, as if she knew it would be empty.

He bit back a curse because he didn't want to scare the kids but, *vaffanculo*, anyone could be in here.

Turns out there was someone here.

He grabbed for the girl but she got away from him and ran straight for the bed.

Fucking hell.

Another girl sat up in the bed, moving slowly, as if from a drugged sleep, her body heavy.

Son-of-a-fucking-bitch.

Pregnant. She was pregnant. His gaze flew to her face and he bit back even worse curses.

She didn't look much older than Amy. And at least six months pregnant, if not more.

Fuck.

Swallowing the bitter venom that wanted to spew from his mouth about the type of cretins who'd impregnate a girl her age, he watched silently as the girls communicated with their hands. He knew only enough sign language to communicate orders.

They were holding a tense conversation, with the pregnant girl shaking her head constantly.

He opened his mouth but Alex must have sensed what he was going to do and put his hand over his mouth. Turning, Kaisie looked at Alex with raised eyebrows but Alex just shook his head repeatedly, his eyes huge.

He got the hint. No sound. Fine. But they had to move now.

Holding up one hand got the attention of both girls and, now that he got a good look at the pregnant one, his heart dipped. Tinia's teat, she looked like Alex. Not a perfect copy, like Amy for Grace, but enough alike that she and the boy had to be related.

What a fucking clusterfuck this was turning out to be.

With one hand, he pointed to the door, hoping Amy understood what he was saying.

She shook her head and pointed to the other door in the room. The pregnant girl started to shake her head furiously, hands curved over her belly protectively.

He smelled her fear as Amy grabbed her arm and pulled her off the bed. The girl's short hair swung around her chin as she continued to shake her head. Still, she followed Amy to the door, just as Kaisie and Alex did.

Inside the bathroom, Amy pointed at the window.

They were on the second floor. Did she expect them to jump?

No way could Alex or the pregnant girl make it without being injured.

Then he saw why she'd picked this spot for their escape.

The tree was just close enough to reach. If it'd been trimmed even inches, they wouldn't have been able to reach it.

It wasn't all that big but it looked sturdy enough to hold her weight. His and Alex's… Well, they didn't have much of a choice.

And the pregnant girl…

Shit. How the hell was he going to get them out safely?

In the hallway, he heard the faint sound of footsteps. He drew in a deep breath and caught the scents of Nic and Duke.

Thank fuck.

Without waiting to explain, he reached around to shift Alex off his back, handing him to Amy. She reached for her brother and, as soon as she had him, he raced back out to the hall.

Duke caught sight of him as he stuck his head out of the doorway. As Kaisie motioned for him to stay silent, Nic's wolf appeared by Duke's side.

Duke and Nic raced down the hall toward Kaisie and they all made it inside the room just as another scent, one Kaisie didn't recognize, got stronger.

Time to go.

Shutting the door to the bedroom behind him as silently as he could, he pointed to the bathroom, where the kids were huddled together against the far wall.

Duke nearly tripped over his feet as he took in the situation, his gaze flipping to Kaisie's for a brief moment before he looked at Alex and Amy.

Nic ran for the window, his front paws making no sound as he looked out. When he turned back to Duke, he motioned with his head for Duke to come closer.

Kaisie joined them and again had to make a conscious effort not to swear.

Two men stood below, not directly but close enough to fuck with their escape.

Shit.

Duke caught his eye then deliberately looked at Nic. Two guards. Two *lucani*. Didn't seem quite fair to the guards, but Kaisie would have no remorse over killing two *Mal*. He could smell the evil on them.

Kaisie nodded, making the motion for silence. Duke nodded but rolled his eyes. Yeah, Kaisie didn't know how quiet they were going to be. The window didn't open. It was set into the wall and they were going to have to break it to get out.

He looked around for something to break the window with, settled for the stool in the corner.

But as he picked it up and moved back to the window, Amy grabbed his arm. She opened her mouth to speak then closed it tight and held up both hands, fingers spread.

Then she turned to the window, raised her hands with her palms facing the glass. She turned to the pregnant girl for several seconds, as if seeking reassurance. Her arms tight around Alex, the other girl nodded, though fear showed plainly on her face.

Noise in the stairwell from the third floor. Kaisie whipped his head around as he caught the sound of running feet.

With his hand, he motioned for Amy to do whatever she was planning. They'd run out of time.

With a short nod, her mouth firmed and her eyes closed.

Then she drew so much power, Kaisie felt his wolf rise with an almost manic rush.

Before he had time to worry about whether he was going to shift, Amy sent all that power outward.

And blew out the wall.

*****

"Now that you're here, you're going to want to see your children, aren't you? I'm sure you'll agree they're healthy. Our son may be somewhat happy to see you but I don't think our daughter will share his enthusiasm. After all, you did abandon her."

She knew better than to respond to his taunts, even though fury burned in her gut.

The bastard yanked her hair again, hard and she caught John's expression out of the corner of her eye. He was beyond angry and well into pissed but he was holding it together. Plotting to get her away from Ettore.

She caught John's eyes and shook her head, just once. The tight hold Ettore had on her hair made it painful, but she had to get John to stay away. This might be the only way she could see her children. If Kaisie and the rest of the *lucani* had failed…

"Yes, tell the *eteri* not to be stupid." Ettore dragged her closer to the door he'd entered through.

If he got her through that door, there was no way she'd be leaving this building. At least not alive.

And dead would be preferable to what he would do to her. She couldn't live like she had when she'd been with him.

But John wasn't going to let her go without a fight. He leaped off the floor and flew at them.

Grace felt the knife cut into her neck, the pain instant and sharp.

Blessed Goddess, he really was going to kill her.

She had a moment of sheer terror that turned into an icy numbness.

And then the house rocked beneath Grace's feet.

The floor shook, throwing Ettore one way and Grace the other. The blade caught her arm as they both fell, slashing so deep, it nicked the bone. The pain blazed through her like acid, but she bit back a scream as she pushed herself as far away from Ettore as she could manage.

It wasn't far enough.

His features twisted in a snarl, he came after her. "You bitch. What did you do?"

She hadn't done anything. But she believed she knew who had. That explosion could only mean the *lucani* had to blast their way out.

Ettore reached for her but he never got to her. John tackled him.

"Get Kaine and get out!" John yelled just before he hauled back and hit Ettore with a fist to the side of his head.

Yes. Kaine. Get Kaisie's daughter out.

She ran for the wolf, finally coming out of unconsciousness. Kaine shook her head, huffing as she tried to stand. But she gave up with a yip as her left paw folded under her.

Grace gritted her teeth against the pain shooting through her arm and wrapped both of her arms around Kaine. The wolf weighed at least a hundred pounds and her arm screamed bloody murder but she carried the wolf toward the door.

Behind her, she heard the sound of flesh on flesh. John may be *eteri* but he was a trained soldier. Ettore usually surrounded himself with bodyguards who took care of any physical threats. He could throw a few punches but he'd never been a fighter.

She hoped John beat the shit out of him.

Through her labored breathing, she heard shouting but she had no idea what they were saying. The sounds were muted, distorted. She ran for the door they'd entered through and stopped to look out. She reached for the doorknob and nearly screamed as Kaine's weight shifted against her injured arm.

But she couldn't make a sound. Two men ran by the door. Not part of her little party. Must be Ettore's men on their way to wherever the explosion had been.

Okay, that had to mean she'd be able to get Kaine to the rendezvous point and make it back to get her children out.

She looked out the window. Seeing no one, she opened the door with her good hand and bit back a groan. The wound at her neck no longer bled or stung, but damn, her arm hurt. And the blood flow from that wound hadn't slowed. She should be worried about that but there was no time for it.

Instead, she ran as fast as she could for the screen of trees across a half acre of open grass.

* * * * *

Out of the corner of his eye, Kaisie caught sight of a flash of color and movement on the ground to his left.

Alex dangled from his hands out of the hole Amy had blown in the wall. Duke stood on the rubble below, reaching for Alex. The girls had already been lowered and stood against the wall, arms around each other, clinging.

The pregnant one was crying. Though obviously younger, Amy hadn't cracked yet, her expression determined as she stared up at him. Tough girl. And a powerful one.

She willed him to move faster with those dark eyes so like her mother's.

As he dropped Alex into Duke's waiting hands, he turned to look for that flash of movement.

His heart nearly stopped when he realized it was Grace, running from the house with a wolf in her arms.

Kaine. Had to be Kaine. Nic's wolf stood below with Duke and Seth's wolf guarded his back in the bedroom.

Vaffanculo, they were perfect targets. The guards… Where the hell—

There. Two guards rounded the corner of the building farthest from Kaine and Grace but nearer to them.

The men had guns but the *stregone* Kaine had asked to accompany them lifted his hand toward them, drawing power to him in a rush that brushed against Kaisie's *arus,* his magic, like velvet on bark.

Neither gun went off but Kaisie didn't have time to wonder what the *stregone* had done.

"Drop him. Now."

The urgency in Duke's voice registered and Kaisie let go of the boy.

Duke caught Alex and practically tossed him at the *stregone.*

"Get them out of here. Seth, Race!" he called to the men in the room behind him. "Let's go."

The pull of power was so strong this time, Kaisie actually shivered as the *stregone* transported the girls and Alex back to the den in Pennsylvania. He'd never get used to seeing people disappear right in front of his eyes but he didn't have time to dwell on it now.

Marrucini's men had reached them. And they were pissed.

And well trained.

Fists and legs flew, wolves' jaws snapped and growls split the air.

Kaisie got clocked in the head with a lucky swing from one of the two men trying to take him down.

Guess he should be honored he rated two men. Everyone else was paired off with one.

The fight devolved into a brawl worthy of a Saturday night at a biker bar, except those guys didn't usually fight with their teeth.

The *lucani* had the advantage but they weren't putting Marrucini's men down fast enough to be able to get away.

One of the guards fell to the ground, knocked out by Duke, who moved over to help Kaisie with his two.

"We need to get out of here now." Duke's quiet voice carried over the noise of the fight.

"I know." Kaisie dodged a fist aimed at his gut and landed his own on his opponent's jaw. "We could shift and run for it but John can't keep up."

"Then we need to give him a head start."

Kaisie nodded, throwing another punch. "Do it."

Duke let himself take a punch to the kidney then stumbled backward. Right into John, who'd burst out of the doorway from the kitchen seconds ago and landed straight in the fight.

Kaisie dodged another punch that came much too close to landing because his attention was fractured.

They had to get out of here…

John broke off from the group and started to run like hell for the trees Grace had disappeared into.

When he was almost there, Kaisie gave the order that he hoped would get them all the hell out of here.

"Commuto."

Chapter Four

"Kaine! Shit. Grace, get in the goddamn van. We're out as soon as they get here."

"She's gonna bleed out. That cut's too deep."

Grace heard John swear and forced herself to open her eyes. But even that much motion made her arm throb in agony, even as the rest of her felt curiously numb.

She bit back a groan and tried to speak. Had to know. "The children. Did the—"

She cried out as John did something that made her arm feel as if it was on fire.

She must have passed out because when she came to, she knew there were more people moving around her.

"Shit, this is— Kaisie, she's coming around. Keep her still."

She sensed motion, even through the fiery ache that used to be her arm. Panic boiled in her lungs, making them constrict until she could barely breathe.

"Grace. Stop struggling. You're hurting yourself." The blatant command in Kaisie's voice pissed her off enough that the panic receded the slightest bit and she could think a little more clearly.

"The children—" She hissed as the van hit a pothole and her arm shifted. When had they started to drive? She fought against the oblivion at the edges of her consciousness. "Kaisie, did you get them?"

"Yeah, we got them."

She forced her eyes open because there was something in Kaisie's voice she didn't like.

His face hovered above hers, looking as if he'd gotten hit with a two-by-four to his face.

"Alex? You got Alex? And my—"

He laid two fingers on her lips. "We got them both. Now shut up and save your strength."

She fought against the lethargy that threatened to take her under again. "How bad's my arm?"

His mouth tightened and his eyes flashed away for a several seconds before returning to hers. "Just stay still."

That bad. She must have lost a lot of blood. "You're not lying about the children, are you?"

His eyes narrowed down to slits of bright green. "You're starting to piss me off, lady. I'm not lying. Just don't fucking move."

"Tell them I love them."

Kaisie leaned even closer, until she could barely focus on him. "You can tell them yourself when we get home."

Home. She liked the sound of that. Even though she knew that home was only temporary. That even though the *lucani* king had sent his men after her children, it didn't mean he'd let them stay forever.

Not her, a former *Mal* pawn, or her daughter, a full-blooded *Mal*. They'd have to run. Find somewhere to hide. Find…

She let her eyes close then, too tired to keep them open any longer.

*****

"The bleeding's stopped but I don't know if it'll be enough until we get home," John said. "She lost a lot of blood."

The pilot had gotten them into the air the second Duke had shut the hatch and locked it. They hadn't lost anyone but Kaine had a broken front leg that would need to be set before she could shift. Seth had a few broken ribs and Race's face looked as if he'd taken a running leap into a stone wall.

Nothing life-threatening. Except for Grace.

"She's gonna need a transfusion when we get back," John continued. "I already contacted Dane and he's calling Nica as well. But… It might be too late, Kaisie. She lost a lot of fucking blood."

He understood what John was saying. He just refused to believe she was going to die.

He looked at Kyle, sitting on the other side of the aisle. "How long until we land?"

Kyle shook his head. "Another ninety minutes. At least."

She wouldn't make it that long.

Tinia's teat. What the fuck should he do?

Helplessness wasn't a state he typically found himself in. The last time he felt it was more than twenty-five years ago when Tekeias, Kaine's mother, had shoved their baby into his arms and told him she couldn't stay. He'd never seen her again. She'd been killed by the *Mal* shortly after that.

Kaisie had panicked. He hadn't had a fucking clue what to do with a baby. And the *lucani* had been in the middle of a war back then. A secret battle against a group of *eteri* fanatics who called themselves Zuhno, an old Romany word that meant pure.

They'd made it their job to wipe out the *lucani*. The *lucani* had fought back and won. But it'd been a long battle and he'd let the den rear his daughter more than he had. He'd felt helpless in the face of her cries and the overwhelming responsibility of caring for a tiny baby utterly dependent on him.

He'd loved his daughter at first sight but at the age of nineteen, Kaisie hadn't known how to juggle his duties as a tracker and his responsibility as a father.

Luckily for him and Kaine, the *lucani* hadn't let him fail her. They'd taken care of her when he'd had to leave and they'd taught him everything he'd needed to know to take care of her himself when he was home. His parents had helped as much as they could but they'd been close to seventy when Kaine had arrived. And gone by the time she was ten.

He looked at his daughter across the aisle, still in her wolf pelt and spread out across two seats. They'd wrapped her paw and given her a shot for the pain from the med-kit and now she slept.

Grace had carried his daughter out of the house with that gash on her arm while John had kept Marrucini busy so they could all get away.

Kaisie met John's solemn gaze. "She'll make it. She's too stubborn not to."

* * * * *

Dr. Dane Dimitriou met them at the private hangar at the airport.

He glanced at Kaine before he said she could wait to be seen back at the den by their resident veterinarian, Ryan Maguire.

Kaisie watched Dane's face tighten as he examined Grace before he started hooking her up to tubes and packets.

"We need to get her back to the den. I need to close that wound. She's lost a lot of blood."

Kaisie wished everyone would just stop saying that. He knew she'd lost a lot of blood. It coated her clothes and his. And John's.

"Then let's get moving."

Dane nodded, though his lips flattened almost to the point of disappearing. "Alex is weak and the pregnant girl was having contractions when they showed up. And the other girl, Grace's daughter..." He shook his head. "You let her keep a loaded gun."

Kaisie shrugged his shoulders as he gathered Grace into his arms to get her off the plane. He kept her as still as he could and almost didn't want to put her down on the stretcher Dane had waiting at the bottom of the steps.

"The gun made her feel safe."

"Yeah, well, next time, take the damn bullets away first. She put one in the floor when I tried to take Alex into the exam room without her. We ended up putting Alex and the girl in the same room so Amy could be with both of them." The edges of Dane's mouth curled up. "She's strong. A lot like her mother."

The drive passed excruciatingly slowly. Grace never regained consciousness and, by the time they got to the den, his jaw felt close to shattering.

They carried her and Kaine into the den's medical facility and Dane immediately went to work. Kyle's mate, Tam, rushed in from somewhere and they started to talk in their own language, which sounded like English but didn't make a damn bit of sense to Kaisie.

He could only watch as they started to work.

"Kaisie, why don't you go check on Kaine?"

Kaisie lifted his gaze to Dane's and started to shake his head before Kyle put his hand on Kaisie's shoulder.

"Come on, man," Kyle said. "Someone will come get you if something happens. Kaine's awake. She needs you. And you should check on the kids. The girl's asking for you. And you need to tell her to put the gun away. She's scaring the natives."

"Amy. Her name's Amy."

"Great. Tell Amy she needs to give you the gun. No one's going to hurt her here."

But they wouldn't hesitate to separate and confine her if she did attempt to hurt someone and that might push her over the edge right now.

With a nod, Kaisie turned and headed down the hall to the exam rooms, using his senses to guide the way. They weren't difficult to find. The bitter scent of fear drew him to the right room.

He knew Amy had sensed someone coming because when he looked through the window in the door, he saw her sitting at the edge of the bed closest to the door, gun pointed straight ahead.

He couldn't help but smile. He liked this girl. He liked her style.

"Oh, thank the goddess." Nica Donato stopped at his side, just out of range of the window. "I want to check the pregnant girl but the little one with the gun won't let me near her. Said she'd only talk to you."

Kaine glanced at the *strega,* seeing the relief in the pretty brunette's eyes. An Etruscan witch who had the power to heal with her hands, Nica had a quiet disposition and soft smile that made her one of the least threatening-looking people in the world. But he didn't blame Amy for being overly cautious. Growing up in a pit of *Mal* would make anyone paranoid.

"Give me a few minutes," he told Nica.

"The girl's been having contractions and I need to examine her to determine how far along she is and if this is false labor or we need to prevent her from going into labor. Time's not on our side, Kaisie."

"I just need a couple of minutes."

He hoped. Deliberately taking his time opening the door, he walked into the room with both hands at his sides, loose and open. Amy kept the gun trained on him as he closed the door behind him, deliberately turning his back to her for several seconds.

When she didn't shoot him in it, he figured that was a good sign. He walked over to stand in front of her as she scrambled to her feet, never taking the gun off him.

"I'm gonna need you to put that away now, Amy. Your friend needs to be checked out." He turned to Alex on the other bed. "Hey, bud. How you feeling?"

The kid smiled, relief in every relaxed line of his body. "Better now that we're ho—here."

Kaisie nodded, returning the smile. "Good. Did you tell Amy we're not going to hurt you guys?"

He nodded, his smile fading. "Yeah. But she's worried."

Kaisie looked back at Amy, noticing the fine tremor in her arms now. The weight of the gun was getting heavier. "I get that. I do. But I promise you, no one will hurt you here. But you've got to be willing to put down the gun. Your friend needs to be checked out. Can she speak?"

Amy worried her bottom lip between her teeth for several seconds before she lowered the gun to her side. "No. She can't hear either. And she's our cousin. Her name's Mara. She's seven months pregnant."

Kaisie nodded. "Okay, Amy. Now, will you give me the gun so—"

"No." She had it pointed at him in a flash. "No. I know what you think of people like me. I know the first chance you get you'll throw me in a dark hole somewhere. But I promised Mara that everything will be okay and—"

Kaisie moved so fast, Amy didn't have time to get off a shot before he took the gun out of her hand. He saw fear leap onto her face and heard twin gasps of shock from behind him.

Tears leaped into Amy's eyes before she blinked them away then stood even straighter as if waiting for him to hit her.

With a few movements, he unloaded the half-full clip, made sure there was none in the chamber and shoved the bullets in his pocket. Then he flipped the gun in his hand and held it back out to Amy.

Confusion bled through the fear now as she took the gun.

"It won't shoot but it'll hurt like hell if you use it to hit someone. But you won't need to. Not here. We do not hurt kids."

Was he getting through to her? He couldn't tell but it didn't matter. The other girl, Mara, had sucked in a deep breath and was starting to pant.

"Now, your cousin needs help. Are you gonna let the *strega* in without a fight?"

Amy's mouth firmed and she nodded then folded herself into the corner closest to Mara. The wary fear he'd seen at the house had returned.

He wanted that gone from her face but he realized it would take time. Time they might never get if Cole decided the girl was a threat.

Without taking his gaze from Amy's, he motioned for Nica to enter. She headed straight for the bed and started asking questions.

Which, of course, Mara couldn't hear.

"You're gonna need to translate, kid. No one but you knows sign language."

Her sneer returned. "You trust me enough for that?"

Kaisie smiled at her bravado. "For that, yeah. Come on, do your thing and help out your cousin."

With a nod, Amy went to shove the gun at her back before realizing she still wore her nightgown.

She looked down at herself, disgust all over her face before she took a deep breath and set the gun on the floor between her feet and looked at Nica.

Nica immediately began asking questions. What was her due date? Had she had any complications? How close together were the contractions?

Kaisie stepped over to Alex. "Come on, bud. I don't think you wanna be in here for this."

Picking up the boy, he moved to the door and looked back at Amy. "You have my word nothing will happen to him and you'll see him later." He made sure the girl looked him in the eyes before he headed out the door. "And I'll find you some clothes. Everything's gonna be okay."

He left before she could contradict him.

*****

Grace woke with one hell of a headache.

She opened her eyes but snapped them closed at the blast of bright light.

Groaning, she tried to lift her arm to put her hand over her eyes but found she couldn't lift it.

Was she tied to a bed? Her eyes flew open, the light not as bright this time but still enough to bring tears to her eyes.

A huge dark shadow moved across her, blocking the light.

"Hey, Grace. It's okay. You're fine. Your arm's immobilized. That's all. You're safe."

She knew that voice. "Kaisie."

"Yeah. Alex is fine. So is Amy."

"Amy?"

"Your daughter. Alex is in the next room. He finally fell asleep about an hour ago but he fought it for a while. I didn't think you'd want him to see you until you woke up."

"Thank you." It was exactly what she would have wanted. As her eyes finally adjusted to the light, she realized the room was dark, the only light coming from what she assumed was the bathroom to the left of the bed.

She blinked, bringing Kaisie's face into focus. He looked…tired. As if he hadn't slept in days. She wanted to ask why he looked so awful but caught the words before they escaped. "Are they okay? Alex and…and Amy?"

"They're fine. I left Amy with Mara to translate."

"Mara? Translate?" Her brain must still be partially asleep because she had no idea what he was talking about.

"Amy said Mara is her cousin. She looks a lot like Alex, so I'm guessing she's right about that. How are you feeling?"

The question threw her for a moment. She wanted more information, more answers to all the questions rolling around in her head. Blinking up at him, she realized her arm hurt but the pain felt dull. As if it'd been masked.

"What happened..." She looked down at her arm. "Ettore cut me."

"He cut you pretty bad."

Her gaze flew back to Kaisie's. That sounded almost like a growl. "I guess it couldn't have been that bad. I'm still here."

"You nearly died."

She frowned at the tone of his voice. He sounded angry. "Why are you mad?"

"I'm not— Okay, yeah, I'm mad. How the hell did he get that close to you?"

Her eyes widened at the menace in his tone, though it didn't feel directed at her. He was pissed but not at her. "Kaine was injured. I needed to give John time to get to her."

She watched Kaisie's eyes close for a few seconds as the muscles in his jaw clenched in a way that looked quite painful. She wanted to cup his cheek and kiss that muscle.

And even though they'd had sex, she couldn't believe he'd want her to touch him.

She swallowed and let her gaze drop. "How's Kaine? Is she okay?"

"Kaine's fine. You nearly died."

"But I didn't."

He looked ready to say something else then must have decided against it because his jaw did that muscle-jumping thing again. "Would you have cared if you had?"

"How would I have known?"

She had no idea what he was getting at and it was frustrating the hell out of her trying to figure out his mood. Was he angry because his daughter had been hurt? Because Grace had caused trouble with her injury? Had they lost someone in the raid?

"Did everyone… Is everyone okay? Did everyone make it back?"

"Yes. And you were the only one who was hurt."

Okay, now she was starting to get angry, which made her head hurt. Whatever they'd done to her arm to make it numb, it didn't extend to her head.

She lifted her good hand to her temple and rubbed the ache there. "Kaisie—"

"No. *Shit.*" He released a hard sigh and shook his head. "Forget it. I'll go get Alex. I promised him I'd wake him as soon as you opened your eyes."

She tried to reach for him but she forgot her arm was tied down and she wrenched it hard against the restraint. Now that hurt and she couldn't stop her groan of pain.

"Gods damn it, woman. Dane said you had to keep it immobile."

"Then don't walk away from me when I'm trying to talk to you, you stubborn *scassacazzo*."

His gaze flashed back to hers as she called him a pain in the ass, which wasn't exactly where she hurt right now but it was close enough.

"Release my arm."

His arms crossed over his chest. "Dane said you can't move it."

"I won't move it. Just, please let my arm go. I don't like being restrained."

The break in her voice at the end of that sentence probably revealed more than she'd wanted. His gaze began to burn with an unholy fire and she dropped hers to watch as he removed the cuffs holding her arm in place. His fingers shook but he released her without touching her at all.

Before he could move, she grabbed one of his wrists with her good arm, feeling his pulse jump beneath her fingers. "Thank you. For everything."

He sighed and shook his head as he stared down at her. "Don't. I'm no fucking hero."

Then he turned and strode toward the door.

She released the breath frozen in her lungs in a slow stream through her lips. Yes, he was. To her.

She wished she could say it without him thinking she was merely talking about the way he'd rescued her children. She'd have to ask him the particulars at another time. She needed to know what had happened.

Had John killed Ettore? If so, would the *Mal* retaliate? If not, would Ettore? He'd taken her son for a specific reason, otherwise, he wouldn't have bothered. Ettore had no use for a sick child.

If he lived, he'd definitely be coming after Amy. She liked the name, even though he'd chosen it for her. She couldn't wait to see her. Wondered if her daughter looked at all like her or if she favored Ettore. The girl probably hated her. She shouldn't get her hopes up for a loving reunion. Who knew what lies Ettore had told the girl about her.

She hadn't even asked if the girl had left willingly.

Guess she'd find out soon enough.

The door opened again and she nearly burst into tears.

She managed to hold them back as Kaisie set Alex on the bed by her good arm. Still asleep, her little man looked no worse for wear as he curled against her.

She tried to speak but didn't think she could without sobbing. So she buried her nose in her baby's hair and pretended she wasn't.

*****

Kaisie left, figuring she'd want the time alone with Alex. Besides, he could smell her tears and he didn't think she'd want him to see those.

Heading back down the hall, he knocked first then pushed open the door into the room the girls were in.

Nica smiled tiredly at him from the side of the bed, where she sat with her hand resting on Mara's swollen belly. On the other bed, Amy lay with her back to the room, curled in around herself. Asleep. Or so she wanted them to believe.

He'd let her get away with the deception for now. Hell, the kid had earned some downtime.

"How's she doing?" He nodded at Mara, deeply asleep.

"I've managed to get the contractions stopped but she's close to eight months pregnant according to Amy. Dane's going to do an ultrasound when she wakes but I believe the baby's far enough along to be born without complications."

"And they're both healthy?"

"Mara's been very well taken care of." Nica's face twisted in an ugly grimace. "Of course, they put a spell over her so they wouldn't have to hear her cry or have her hear what they were saying. But then we are talking about the *Mal*."

His eyes widened. "You're fucking kidding me?"

Nica's mouth flattened into a cold hard line. "No. I was able to get that much out of Amy before she clammed up and told me to mind my own business. The girl's got balls. Guess you'd have to grow up *Mal*. But…"

"But what?"

Nica sighed as she removed her hand from Mara's belly and stood, stretching out her back. Then she motioned for Kaisie to follow her to the far corner of the room, where she thought she'd be out of hearing range.

"There's something different about Amy," Nica said. "Something I can't put my finger on but there's definitely something…off with her."

"You mean something other than being *Mal*."

Nodding, her gaze went over Kaisie's shoulder to the girl still pretending to be asleep. "I can sense that part of her, that darkness that makes her *Mal*, but then…there's something else beneath it. I just don't know how to explain it."

"Is she sick? Like Alex."

Nica shook her head. "No, she's perfectly healthy. It's… Hell, it's like a shadow underneath everything else she is. That's the only way I know how to describe it and that's not doing a very good job."

"Did you ask her about it?"

"No. The girl's exhausted. I don't think she's been able to sleep more than a few hours a night for the past few months. And maybe less since Alex's abduction. I think she took on the job as Mara and Alex's protector and…" Nica tried unsuccessfully to stifle a huge yawn. "Took the job seriously."

Kaisie didn't have to think that's what had happened. He knew it. "Why don't you go get some sleep? I'll sit with the girls."

Nica didn't put up a fight. "Thanks, Kaisie. If Mara wakes and complains of back pain or cramps, come and get me right away. I'll be in the next room."

"Got it."

Nica's gaze landed on Amy again then she shook her head. "That girl's got a backbone of steel. What the hell are we going to do with her, Kaisie? She's got wicked-strong power."

And she's *Mal*. Nica didn't have to add that last bit. They both knew that was the elephant sitting in the middle of the room. Or lying on the bed.

Nica gave him one last tired smile then headed out the door.

Kaisie waited a full minute before he walked over to Amy's bed. "You can roll over now. I know you're awake."

Amy rolled to her back, one arm behind her head, the other over her stomach as she stared up at him. That look was back, the stubborn set of her mouth that Kaisie recognized. From her mother.

"You really need to get some sleep, little girl. You'll be no good for your cousin if you can't keep your eyes open."

"Mara may need me. I'm her eyes and ears now."

"So I understand." He drew the chair by the wall to the side of the bed and sat down as Amy watched his every move. "You wanna tell me what happened to her?"

Amy's sneer would have done Grace proud. "You wanna know about how my loving father put a spell on his niece so he wouldn't have to hear her cry or worry about her overhearing his plans for her and the baby? About how, if the baby was born *Mal*, he'd be able to get a much better price for Mara the next time?"

Kaisie's blood ran cold at the flat, dead sound of Amy's voice, though he struggled not to show his disgust. He had a feeling she'd clam up if he did. And that was the last thing he wanted her to do.

"So you both learned sign language."

She shrugged, as if there'd been nothing else she could do. "Mara needed me."

"Was she born *Mal*, too?"

"No, but her father is. He's my father's brother. I guess that makes him my uncle." She said the word like a curse. "My father brought her to live with us four years ago. Mara said her parents told her they'd done everything they could for her and now she needed to earn her keep. She was sixteen."

Kaisie had to work hard to keep his teeth from grinding. He just nodded at Amy, knowing she was watching his reactions, looking for any hint of softness so she could dismiss him as unworthy.

"A year ago, Mara fell in love with one of our bodyguards. She thought he loved her. She got pregnant. And found out my father had orchestrated the whole thing. The guy was the son of one of my dad's business partners. And *Mal*. Father was so pleased she got knocked up so fast. And when Mara found out she'd been used, she cried for three days straight until he brought in an old hag to cast a spell to take away her hearing and her voice. She's been like this for the past six months."

Staring into Amy's deep-brown eyes, Kaisie sincerely hoped the bastard hadn't died because he wanted the pleasure of torturing the man for days until he took his last agonized breath. He had the feeling Amy wished she could do the same.

Which just added to his fury. No fifteen-year-old girl should ever have to go through this nightmare.

"If Mara okays it, we'll have our *streghe* take a look at the spell. See if they can break it without harming her."

Amy nodded, a short, sharp motion that was almost military. "And what about me? What are you going to do with me? I'm *Mal*."

No hint of any emotion whatsoever in her eyes. The girl had her emotions locked down tight. And who could blame her, the way she'd been reared?

"You were born *Mal*, yes. But you heard what Nica said before she left. Wanna tell me what she meant about that shadow she senses in you?"

Now fear flared for a brief second before she could hide it. "I don't know what she's talking about."

Yeah, she did, but now probably wasn't the time to push about that. "What about your powers? Obviously you've come into them."

Usually *streghe* came into their powers with their first period, which made for a hell of a wicked month. *Lucani* girls' first change hit when their bodies reached a certain maturity level, which didn't always coincide with their cycle. But maybe there was something different about *Mal* powers.

She didn't say anything for so long, he thought maybe she wouldn't open her mouth again. "I have an affinity for stone. And I can make things explode. Apparently I'm quite the trick dog. *Daddy* had such plans for breeding me."

The sarcasm was thick enough to cut with a knife but he could smell her fear and her heartache underlying it.

"You don't have to worry about that, Amy. You won't be going back."

"But I can't stay here either. I'm *Mal*. I know what that means, what people like you think about people like me. I'm dangerous. I'm deadly. And let's not forget evil. I have no soul, right? Isn't that what you and the rest of the Etruscans believe?"

Yeah, it was. Because it was mostly true. Although he didn't believe they were born without a soul. He believed they had that beaten out of them.

Which totally sucked when you were staring into the face of a fifteen-year-old girl who knew exactly what you were thinking.

"You didn't ask to be born *Mal*."

"Doesn't matter, does it? Doesn't change the fact that that's what I am. What I'll always be." She shook her head. "I can't stay here. You know that."

Also true. Shit. "We're getting ahead of ourselves. Why don't we table that discussion for another time?"

She shook her head again. "Doesn't matter when we talk about it, the facts'll still be the same. I don't know what my father wanted with Alex. I only know it wasn't because he wanted to get to know the son he'd thrown away because he wasn't born *Mal*. And I know if my father's still alive, he'll be coming for us. And he won't stop until he gets us back."

"The *lucani* aren't afraid of the *Mal,* little girl. We're stronger, faster and there are more of us. If he comes after you, he better be prepared for a war."

Her eye brows lifted. "Didn't you lose the last war you fought with the *Mal*?"

He released the smile he'd been holding back until now, the one that scared grown men. "Honey, that was almost two hundred years ago. Trust me, we've learned a few tricks since then. Now that we've stalled long enough, why don't you let me introduce you to your mother?"

Chapter Five

The girl standing beside her bed had her face.

Grace tried not to appear dumbstruck. Or allow tears to well in her eyes. Or to jump out of bed to grab the girl, dressed in too-baggy shorts and a t-shirt that practically drowned her delicate frame, who stopped just inside the door to her room and refused to come any closer.

"Grace," Kaisie's voice rumbled through the room, "this is Amy. Amy, this is Grace Bellasario."

Grace knew she looked like crap, with her puffy, bloodshot eyes and her messy hair. Her complexion had to be white because exhaustion was starting to seep through her and she felt sick to her stomach with anxiety.

She forced herself to smile, shifting Alex's sleeping body closer as she tried to rearrange herself so she was sitting up.

"Hello, Amy. How are you feeling?"

The girl shrugged, hands deep in the pockets of the shorts, her mouth set in uncompromising lines, as if she hadn't been through a hell of fear in the past twenty-four hours. "I'm fine. How's Alex?"

"He seems fine. Kaisie told me you took care of him. I want to…to thank you for that."

Amy's head tilted back the tiniest bit but her expression didn't change. "He's my brother."

As if that meant more than anything in the world to her. Much more than a mother who'd abandoned her to be reared by a monster.

"Yes, he is."

An awkward silence fell as Grace tried to find the right words, the words that wouldn't send her daughter running. But everything she wanted to say, everything she *needed* to say would sound like excuses. And this girl with her eyes and the same stubborn expression on her face deserved more than excuses.

"Were you injured at all in the escape?"

Amy shook her head, her gaze dropping to Grace's bandaged arm. "Were you?"

"Just a cut. It'll be fine."

"Good."

"Would you like—"

"Can I go back to my room now?" Amy addressed her question to Kaisie and Grace felt the cut as deeply as she had the one Ettore had made with the knife. "I think I wanna get some sleep now. I'm kinda tired."

Grace forced a smile, nodding. "Of course. When you wake, I'm sure Alex will be glad to see you."

"Sure." She shrugged. "Tell him I'll check in with him."

Then Amy looked at Kaisie, as if for permission, before she turned and disappeared through the door.

Two minutes. Had it even been two minutes? She hadn't even gotten to touch her.

Grace's vision blurred but she blinked back the tears. She had to be stronger than this. She'd known it was going to take more than a few minutes to undo fifteen years of Ettore's influence.

And she wasn't a quitter.

A dark shadow appeared over her. Kaisie, reaching down to take Alex.

"No, don't—"

"Shh, Grace." His voice whispered along her senses. "I'm just moving him to the other bed. I'm not taking him out of the room. Hang tight. I'll be right back."

That voice made her chest ache. Her good hand clenched into a fist in her lap as Kaisie laid Alex on the bed next to hers, only inches away. Alex was so deeply asleep, he didn't make a sound or move a muscle when Kaisie drew the covers over him.

Her gaze stayed locked on Alex as Kaisie walked around to the far side of her bed, as if he knew she didn't want him between her and Alex. Or maybe he just wanted to be closer to the door so he could leave that much faster. Like her daughter.

"She hates me."

She hadn't meant to say anything. Definitely hadn't meant to sound so…despairing.

"Grace."

She ignored him, ignored the command in his tone. He wanted her to look at him. She kept her eyes glued to the sheet covering her lap.

"I think I'd like to be alone now. Please leave."

"Yeah, that's not gonna happen."

She held on to the threads of her temper by sheer force of will. She couldn't afford to blow her cool now. She had to keep it together. The *lucani* had been good to her. But she couldn't afford to overstay her welcome. She had to take her children and get the hell away from here.

Before Ettore sent his people to take back his children and laid waste to everything in his path.

She forced herself to lift her gaze and meet his steady, dark eyes. "Thank you for everything you've done for my children. We should be out of your hair in a week, maybe less."

The man's gorgeous mouth tilted up, his eyes crinkled and he started to laugh. The bastard actually laughed at her.

Her back straightened and the tears dried in her eyes. "What exactly are you laughing at? None of this is funny."

"You thinking you're going to be leaving in a week is funny as all hell, woman. Where do you think you're going to go? Amy won't leave Mara behind and Mara's almost ready to give birth so she's not going anywhere. Alex likes it here. And admit it. So do you. Aren't you sick of running yet? Besides, you'd miss me if you left."

Every word was a jackhammer at her bruised heart. Every single word true. Except that last statement. Of course she wouldn't miss him.

She wouldn't miss his gorgeous face or those luminous green eyes or his strength. Or the way he'd made love to her that one stolen night that seemed so far away now. But had been less than two days ago.

A night she'd love to repeat.

Hell, right now, she'd settle for a few stolen minutes held in his arms. She felt so safe there.

Gods damn him. Why did he confuse her so badly? Why was he hanging by her bedside as if he cared about her?

She'd expected that one night to be all she'd ever have with him. She hadn't expected him to declare his undying love. Not for a woman like her.

Yet here he was, telling her she'd miss him.

Which was so true.

And he was right about the other points as well. Where could she take her children and Mara where Ettore or the *Mal* wouldn't find them?

Had she merely traded one prison for another? Why had the *lucani* allowed her to drag them into her battle?

"Why?" She shook her head as she spoke that one simple word.

Kaisie had stopped laughing but he still wore the ghost of a smile. "If you have to ask, you're not ready for the answer." He paused, his smile disappearing completely. "And now you need to stop obsessing for a few hours and get some sleep."

"I don't thi—"

He leaned forward, captured her chin in his hand and pressed his mouth over hers, cutting off whatever she'd been about to say. He kissed her, lips closed, eyes open. A promise. A threat.

That kiss sapped the strength, the fight, right out of her. When he pulled away, she sank back into the pillow.

Her good hand was halfway to her lips but she forced it back down to her side.

Strangely, now she thought maybe she could sleep.

"Go to sleep. The entire mess will be here when you wake. And so will I."

* * * * *

"Yeah, this is gonna go real well."

Kaisie didn't bother to turn toward the door. He knew who stood there so he just gave the guy the bird over his shoulder.

"Still such pleasant manners." Aule's voice was barely audible and Grace and Alex didn't stir. "I hear everything went according to plan."

"Mostly."

"So you plan to keep her or what?"

Fucking Aule. "She's not a pet."

"No. She's definitely a woman. Who you seem unable or unwilling to leave alone."

He thought about his answer for a few seconds before he said what he'd felt since the first moment he'd seen her. "She's mine."

Aule had no immediate snappy comeback for that one and Kaisie finally turned to look at his old friend. Who just raised his eyebrows and stared back at him.

"Nothing to say?"

A grin ghosted around Aule's mouth. "What would you like me to say?"

Kaisie sighed, unfolding himself from the chair he hadn't left for more than a few minutes since Grace had fallen asleep. Almost eight hours ago.

He'd slept some, but mostly he'd just sat here. Thinking.

Yeah, enough of that.

With a nod at Aule, he pushed through the door and out into the hallway. His leg muscles nearly sang with relief as he stretched out the kinks.

"So," Aule said when they'd reached the back door at the end of the hall, "you wanna talk about it or do you just wanna go for a run and exhaust yourself so you don't have to think about it for a while?"

"Think about what?"

"What you're going to do about her."

Kaisie looked his friend straight in the eyes. "There's nothing to think about."

Aule nodded. "Okay. So you're just gonna tell her she's moving in and you and her and the kids will live happily ever after. Barring an attack by the *Mal* who want to kill you and her and take the kids away to become evil."

Leaning against the wall, Kaisie shoved his hands in his jeans. "When did you become a fucking cynic?"

"I'm a romantic compared to you. *Vaffanculo*, Kaisie, next you're gonna tell me it was love at first sight."

"I'm forty-four fucking years old, Aule. I'm not some witless kid thinking with his dick." He paused, sighing as he ran a hand through his hair. "I know what the hell I want. And it's not like we haven't spent any time together. We spent an entire week together."

"Fighting. You spent most of the week fighting."

"We didn't kill each other. She's a strong woman. I like that."

"What about sex? Do you like that too?"

"Sure. It was great."

Aule's mouth actually dropped open. "When— Oh hell, never mind. I should've known. Tinia's teat, Kaisie. What do you want me to say?"

"Hell. Fuck if I know. Tell me I'm not being an idiot."

"That's the one thing no one can say about you. You're definitely not an idiot." Aule shook his head, his mouth finally curving in a smile. "Shit, Kaisie. You sure know how to do things up right."

"It's a gift."

"Just something to think about, but…does the lady return your affections?"

Kaisie thought about flipping Aule off again for trying to yank his chain then figured it would be wasted on the guy. "I believe she could be persuaded to do so, yeah."

"You mean you're gonna woo her."

"What the fuck does that mean, anyway? Shit, we're not kids anymore. I want her. She wants me. Why the hell can't we just admit it and move on to spending the rest of our probably short lives together?"

Aule's incredulous expression made Kaisie want to hunch his shoulders like a disgraced teenager. "Seriously? Have you always been this clueless about women or did you get your head knocked in on the mission? Uni's ass, Kaisie, please tell me you're kidding?"

"Why would I?"

Aule started to laugh again, keeping it low as he shook his head. "Buddy, you are in for a seriously rude awakening."

Kaisie crossed his arms over his chest and stared down at his best friend, who could barely keep his laughter from braying out all over the fucking place. "Then tell me, Casanova. What *should* I be doing?"

Throwing his arm around Kaisie's shoulders, Aule pulled him toward the door. "Let's go for a walk. This could take a while."

* * * * *

When she woke again, Grace felt much more human than she had when she'd fallen asleep.

No light seeped through the shade at the window, so it had to be after eight p.m. and before seven a.m. On the bed next to hers, Alex continued to sleep.

Looking around, she saw no one else.

And she refused to believe she was upset that he wasn't here.

He'd told her—

The door opened and her breath caught in her chest as Kaisie walked into the room, a covered tray in his hands.

Damn it. Just...damn it. He looked so tall and strong, dressed in faded jeans and a plain dark t-shirt. He still hadn't shaved but she had to admit he looked damn good with that dark stubble on his face, she hoped he kept it.

And those green eyes made her heart pound.

She refused to believe she was going to cry just because he'd returned. He'd said he'd be here when she woke and, Gods damn it, here he was.

Damn him.

"Hey, how're you feeling?"

And damn that voice for making her blood heat. "Much better, thank you."

His eyes narrowed at her stilted tone but he just kept coming. The aroma of grilled meat from the tray made her stomach growl and sent a flush into her cheeks.

Setting the tray on the table next to her, he surprised the hell out of her by bending to press a kiss to her forehead.

Another one of those quick, hard kisses that shouldn't leave her breathless. And confused. But it did.

"So I hope you like hamburgers." He pushed the button on the side of the bed to elevate the backrest. "And salad and vegetable soup. I swiped some chocolate cake too but you need to eat the rest before you can have that. I'm pretty handy with the grill but Aule's wife made the cake. She's hell on wheels in the kitchen."

She looked at the tray then back to him, not knowing what to say. Even if she could get it through the lump in her throat. Instead she nodded and dipped her head so he couldn't see her expression as she reached for the tray. Before she could, he had the legs extended and set the tray over her lap.

Having no idea who Aule was, she merely nodded and reached for the cover on the tray. But he was there first, again, and whipped it away. The scent of the food nearly made her swoon. Almost as much as his kiss had and she felt a smile tug at her mouth.

"Thank you."

Out of the corner of her eye, she caught his shrug. "You haven't eaten anything for way too long. You need to get your strength back."

All the better to be able to leave faster. Since she didn't want to start another fight, she merely nodded and started to dig in. She nearly embarrassed herself by moaning over the juicy taste of the burger. The man hadn't exaggerated his grill efficiency.

"No change with Mara," he reported as he sat in the chair next to her bed. "Both girls are asleep right now. Mara hasn't had any more contractions so Nica thinks she might be able to go at least another week, which will be better for the baby. Make sure you eat everything."

She nodded as he fell silent. When she peeked over at him as she switched from the burger to the soup, she saw he'd closed his eyes and rested his head on the chair back, looking completely at ease.

With a shake of her head, she let herself eat until she was sated, the first meal she'd had in what felt like years that wasn't bolted down because she had to be somewhere else or an afterthought because she had to make sure Alex was eating.

She couldn't finish everything but she did manage to eat most of the chocolate cake. Kaisie was right. It tasted like heaven on a fork.

Her eyes closed in ecstasy and she couldn't contain her nearly breathless groan. She sneaked a peek at Kaisie to make sure he hadn't heard and found him asleep.

He didn't look any softer in sleep, she realized. Still tough, strong. Handsome.

Sighing, she lowered her fork to the tray, careful not to make any sound to wake him. He didn't look exhausted but she had the feeling he hadn't slept since they'd returned, which had to be at least twenty-four hours ago.

He'd been too busy. Checking on her daughter. Checking on Alex. Feeding her.

If she let herself, she might think he cared for her. Which was utterly ridiculous.

And totally sigh-worthy.

And completely confusing.

What did he want from her?

As if he'd heard her question, his eyes opened. He couldn't have been asleep more than fifteen minutes, but he looked clear-eyed and alert.

"I can practically hear you thinking, Grace. Does your brain ever stop?"

"Not really, no," she answered honestly. "I understand it can be totally annoying."

He shrugged. "Could be. For someone with an inferiority complex. Luckily I don't have one."

She didn't bother to hide her smile, though she contained her laughter. "No, that's one thing I don't think anyone could accuse you of."

"That smile's a killer, you know. You should be careful how you use it."

Well hell. What should she say to that? It almost sounded as if he was flirting but that couldn't be right. Maybe he was being sarcastic and she was reading him wrong.

Or maybe he really was flirting with her, in which case, she still didn't know what to say. She had no experience with flirting.

She wanted to ask him what he meant, how he felt about her. Gods, she was awful at this man-woman stuff.

His lips curved in a wry grimace. "And I should have kept my mouth shut." He sighed. "Okay, so… I figure since both of us are no longer kids, this shouldn't be such a production."

She blinked at him, trying to figure out where he was going with this. Maybe her brain wasn't as clear as she'd thought. "What shouldn't be such a production?"

"And then," he continued on as if she hadn't spoken, "I thought, well, then what's the point?"

"The point of what? Kaisie, what—"

"The point of starting a relationship."

Her mouth opened but nothing came out.

"Huh. Guess your brain does stop occasionally."

Actually, her brain was speeding ahead at a hundred miles an hour. Relationship. Was he actually talking about a relationship between the two of them?

Her heart began to pound as well. And desire spread through her body like a fire.

"Anyway," Kaisie continued, "if we're going to do this, I guess we should do it right. So, I'm giving you a couple of days to recover, get the kids settled, think about what you want to do for the rest of your life. Then I'm going to have you over to my house for dinner. No kids. Just the two of us. I'll cook. We'll talk. Maybe we'll have more great sex, because, babe, the sex was great. Maybe we'll just make out because, technically, it'll only be our first date and I seem to recall there're rules about dating."

"Dating."

His lips curved again and heat flooded through her gut and lower, into her sex. She realized her mouth was hanging open but she couldn't seem to get it to close.

"You want to date me?"

He shook his head. "No. I wanna mate you. But we'll start slow so your brain doesn't explode. And after you get used to me in a few days, we'll work out the details. So..."

He rose, walked over to the bed, leaned close and pressed his lips to hers. Her brain functioned well enough to kiss him back, to tilt her head so he could get a better angle. She felt her lungs shudder and a girly squeak nearly escaped her throat when he pulled away after a too-short kiss.

He stared down into her eyes for several seconds, searching for something. She had no idea what. Dazed and confused didn't come close to what she was feeling at the moment. More like blown away. She couldn't think straight, not with his taste still on her lips and those green eyes still locked with hers.

"You need to sleep. Dane said your body needs rest to heal. Nica's gonna have a go at repairing the damage to your arm tomorrow. Then you should be able to take Alex and Amy back to your house until they get used to us. I'll have to add on a room and another bathroom for the kids at my place eventually. Probably get started on that later this week so it's finished before the weather gets bad in October and November. Kaine and I shared a bathroom but with two kids, I'm guessing we'll need the extra space."

Pulling back, he pressed one index finger under her chin to close her still-open mouth. "Don't worry, babe. I'm pretty handy. The renovations will be done before you know it. Get some more sleep now. I gotta catch a few hours myself but I'll be back before you miss me. Sleep well, Gracie."

Then he left without looking back.

She consciously had to force her mouth closed as the door shut behind him.

The man was crazy. He must have hit his head during the rescue. He couldn't actually be serious.

What the hell did a man like him want with someone like her?

And wouldn't it be lovely if it were true?

* * * * *

"I know it's small, but until we figure out what our next step is, we'll just have to make do."

Grace opened the door into the tiny home she'd been staying in before they'd gone to rescue Alex and Amy and walked into the living room.

Glancing behind her, she saw Amy step into the house, her gaze checking out everything.

As if she wanted to be sure she had all the exit points memorized.

"I thought you could have the bedroom there," Grace pointed to the door leading into the bedroom next to hers. "Alex and I can share the other one."

"Or Amy and me could share a room?" Alex's voice held an excitement she'd rarely heard from him. "That would be okay, wouldn't it? Like at— Like before?"

Grace held her breath, waiting to see what her daughter would say

Amy hadn't spoken more than a few words to her since this morning. The *strega*, Nica, had done another round of healing on her arm, smiled at her and declared her good to go. So she'd dressed and told her children they were leaving. Luckily, Kaisie hadn't been around to argue with her.

She'd actually been surprised to find him MIA and tried not to let herself be worried about that.

Now Amy surprised her. "Sure, Alex. We can share a room."

Okay, she'd called that one wrong. Let's see what else she could screw up.

"I thought maybe we could go shopping—"

"Hey, Kaisie." Amy's expression transformed with her smile. It only lasted a few seconds, but it made Grace's heart stop briefly. She wanted the girl to smile longer than a few seconds. "I didn't know you were coming. Are you going to stay for a while?"

And could the girl make it any more obvious she'd rather be anywhere but with Grace?

Not that Grace could blame Amy for being hero-struck. If someone had told her Kaisie could leap tall buildings in a single bound, she wouldn't hesitate to believe it.

But if someone had told her that same man would look at her as if he wanted to strip her naked and toss her on the nearest bed again, well, that would be just a little too much to ask. Because he'd already done it once.

Could he really have feelings for her that were more than physical?

Just the thought that he might made her giddy. Could she allow herself to even consider it?

Gods, she wanted to. But if she let herself dream, and those dreams didn't come true, what then? She had two children to think about now. She couldn't let herself be distracted. Not even when she burned watching the man walk into the house she wouldn't allow herself to think of as her home.

"Actually, I'm here to take you all back to my house. Figured I'd save your mom the hassle of cooking tonight."

"Cool!" Alex chimed in. "Will Kaine and John be there too?"

Seems Alex had joined the Hail-Kaisie-the-Hero campaign as well.

"Yep, they will. And Cat and her parents and a few other people. And your buddies from school, Jason and Mikey. They've been asking about you."

"Really?" Alex's expression lit up as if he'd won the lottery. "That's awesome! Mom, isn't that great? Kaine told me Jason and Mikey were okay but I didn't think they'd want to see me after… you know."

Yes, she knew. After Alex's kidnapping.

Kaisie must have done some slick talking to get the boys' parents to agree to come. If anything had happened to either of those boys, she was sure their parents would have hounded Cole to get rid of her.

She forced a smile, which wasn't as hard as she'd thought it would be because her son looked so damn happy. All because this man had invited them to dinner.

And damn the man because he had her over a barrel. There was no way she could say no.

"It is. Thank you, Kaisie, for inviting us."

His grin said he knew exactly what she'd rather be saying to him. Then again, maybe he didn't know as much as he thought he did.

"You're very welcome. And since I know Amy needs some clothes, I thought I'd drive you guys to the store. Don't get too excited. It's just Target and the grocery store, but I figure we can get everything everybody needs in one stop."

Grace slid a glance at Amy. Target was probably a far cry from the clothes her father had been buying for her but for now it would do.

For years, Grace had shopped in New York City and never looked at a price tag. She'd learned from her mother. And she'd been able to afford it. The trust her grandmother had funded for her had more than enough money to sustain her and the children for years. And she'd carefully hoarded the money Ettore had given her as well. She hadn't had the luxury of being noble about where the money had come from. Only that she had enough to care for Alex. And now for Amy.

"Sure, Target's fine." Amy shrugged as if it didn't matter where she bought clothes. And maybe it didn't. Maybe she wasn't one of those girls who cared what label was sewn into her clothes.

Grace hadn't learned enough about her daughter to know yet.

As if he'd read her mind, Kaisie changed the subject. "Alex, how're the crutches going?"

Her gaze swung back to her son. Dane had started Alex back on his treatment, the serum she'd developed from Dane's mate's blood. Evie had agreed to continue to donate the blood that kept Alex from wasting away from a disease no one had been able to diagnose.

"They're going great." Alex's enthusiasm couldn't be contained and the tears pushed their way to the surface now. He'd been in that damn wheelchair for more than a year and she'd despaired of him ever getting out of it.

Now he was walking with crutches. The daughter she never thought she'd see was in her care. And a man she couldn't stop thinking about, who'd made her feel like a desirable woman instead of a piece of property, stared at her with a look in his eyes that made her believe he wanted to get her alone.

Her head should be spinning. She couldn't let it.

Because it could all come crashing down in seconds when Ettore regrouped and came after the children.

And he would. Kaisie had to know that. She had to take the children underground. Get them away from the den where there were other children who could be hurt.

But she didn't know if there was anywhere she could take the children and Mara that they'd be safe.

"Hey, kids. Why don't you go out and get in the car. Your mom and I will be out in a few."

Amy shot her a quick glance that Grace couldn't read before she headed toward the door. "Come on, Alex, I'll help you get in."

Kaisie waited until the door shut behind the kids before he spoke. "How are you feeling?"

"I'm feeling fine." And physically she was, except for the stress making her head throb. When she shook her head, she felt sharp jolts hit her temples. "This isn't necessary, Kaisie. You don't have to do this. We'll be fine, until…"

He lifted his eyebrows and continued to stare at her, waiting.

Finally, she sighed. "You know we can't stay here. It's not safe for the *lucani* or the kids. We need to disappear, Kaisie. And we need to do it soon."

Crossing his arms over his chest, he raised his eyebrows. "Do you feel better now that you got that off your chest? Can we go shopping now?"

Her hands clenched into fists at her sides and she tried to ignore the urge to throw something at his head. "Damn it, Kaisie, ignoring the situation won't help. We have to leave. I have to take the kids and go."

"Yeah, you do. We're *going* to the store. And tonight you're coming to my house for dinner. And if we're lucky, the kids will fall asleep early and you and I can spend some time alone."

Her mouth opened but her brain wasn't processing fast enough to come up with a response to his wanting to spend time alone with her.

Yes, she wanted that too. Which was just crazy. A relationship between them was crazy. And yet, here he was, acting as if it was a done deal. "You're crazy."

Kaisie shrugged. "Been called it enough to make me think maybe there's something to it. But it doesn't mean I don't know what I want. Which happens to be you. Don't ask me why. Not now. We don't have time to get into it now. We will later, trust me." He shook his head and that wry smile she adored transformed his expression. "I've come to understand you well enough to know you'll probably talk until you're blue in the face. But it won't change how I feel. That's just the way it is."

She wanted to throw her hands in the air then tear out her hair. "I just don't understand."

Sighing, he shoved his hands in the pockets of his jeans. "Grace, do you want me? And be honest because, like I said before, we're not kids anymore. We don't have to be afraid to say it."

The flush on her cheeks when she thought about how much she did want him must have given him his answer because he smiled again, this time the most flat-out-sexy smile she'd ever seen on a man. It literally made her sex clench and her thighs quiver.

She couldn't get her vocal cords to work, however, and she didn't know what she would've said anyway. She didn't think she'd be able to say anything rational.

"I'm gonna take that as a yes. So be forewarned." He leaned toward her, coming so close and yet not close enough. "Try to run and I'll catch you. I'm much faster and I'm motivated. Try to hide and I'll find you. I've got a great nose and you smell fucking great."

Her mouth dropped open at the raw sensuality in his words. No one had ever spoken to her the way he did. Her heart pounded against her ribs and her mouth dried.

"How's your arm?"

She blinked at his abrupt change of subject. "Huh?"

"How does your arm feel?" He spoke slowly, each word distinct.

"Fine. It feels fine."

"Good." He nodded. "I don't want you lifting anything at all. You point, I'll pick it up. Now we better go before the kids wonder where we are."

He wrapped his arm around her shoulders and hustled her out the door.

* * * * *

"So, I guess that didn't suck too badly. See, you're just gonna have to learn to trust me."

Kaisie stood by the dishwasher, piling pots and plates and bowls in haphazardly as Grace sat at the table watching him with narrowed eyes.

"Kaisie, why don't you let me do those? My arm doesn't hurt at all and I feel like I should do something. You cooked. Let me clean up."

Her teeth worried her bottom lip as she followed his hands back and forth from the sink to the dishwasher. He wasn't positive but he thought she had a problem with the way he was loading the dishes.

Probably not orderly enough.

"No, you just sit. Or you could take a cue from the kids and rack out on the couch."

"No, I'm sure they'll be fine there for a little while." But she looked over her shoulder anyway, as if to assure herself that the kids were still there. She'd probably never stop doing that. Couldn't say he blamed her.

When she turned back to him, her expression had softened and he swallowed down the inappropriate surge of lust.

"Thank you for doing this," she said. "For having those little boys here and for inviting Cat for Amy." She sighed and he knew exactly what she was thinking. "Though I don't know that Amy's going to be making too many friends quickly."

Amy had a long way to go to trust anyone. Kyle's daughter, Cat, had tried to engage the girl in conversation because Cat was just that kind of person. But Amy hadn't said more than a few words the entire night. Instead, she'd studied everyone, as if they were opponents on the battlefield. As if every one of them had been out to get her.

"Sure, it's gonna take some time for her to get comfortable here," he said. "She's gonna be looking over her shoulder for a while. And she's gonna question everything anyone says to her. Can't say as I blame her. Besides, she's *Mal*. And that's a whole other battle."

One he hadn't been thinking about too carefully because that was one thing he couldn't fix.

The girl had come into her power. And, if that little example of blowing out the wall at the house had been any indication, her power was huge and deadly.

Grace started to shake her head again, knowing she had to get through to Kaisie. She had to make him understand. "That's why you know we can't stay here. Not for long. She's *Mal*. Eventually…"

Amy's true colors would show.

"She seems to be pretty levelheaded. And she seems to be genuinely attached to Alex and Mara."

Which was an anomaly for a *Mal*. They typically didn't form attachments.

It made her hope for something she shouldn't.

"I never gave it much thought growing up," she continued. "What it meant to be *Mal*. I only knew I wasn't and that made me different. Less. At least in my parents' and grandmother's eyes. They'd hoped I'd be born *Mal*. When I wasn't, they tried again for years but my mother never got pregnant. The *Mal* have never been prolific."

"Thank the Gods for that."

Her mouth twisted in a wry smile. "Yes, I'm sure you would think that way. Of course my grandmother considered my parents a failure so my father has to work that much harder to prove himself to her in business."

"When did you figure out you weren't like them?"

She squashed the smile that wanted to bloom at the certainty in his voice. "Why do you think I did?"

He rolled his eyes. "Because I know you, Grace. You love your kids. You never met Amy but you were ready to trade your life for hers. That makes you a better person than a *Mal* could ever be."

He made her want to be that person. The one he thought he saw in her. Not that he wasn't right. She did love her children. She'd taken one look at Amy and she'd known, no matter what happened, she would love her daughter.

And she certainly felt something for him, more than simple lust. Which she'd never felt before.

"Besides, you have good taste because you definitely have a thing for me."

His arrogant tone should have made her smile. She knew Kaisie well enough by now to know that's what he'd been aiming for. She couldn't do it, though she didn't bother to contradict him. It'd be a lie.

"Damn. I put that look on your face again." With a sigh, he put the last dish in the washer and slapped the door shut. He pressed a button and a slight hum filled the air as he held out his hand to her. "Come with me."

"The kids—"

"Will be fine. We're only going to the back porch. And I had Margie and Cat put an extra couple of protection spells over the place earlier. No one will get in without me knowing about it."

Kaisie watched her contemplate taking his hand. As if the act held so much more meaning than simply letting him lead her to the porch.

And she'd be right. He wanted her to take his hand. To reach for him and follow him.

Trust. He wanted her trust. Would she ever be able to give him what he wanted?

When she reached for him with her uninjured hand and let him pull her to her feet, he controlled his victorious smile, but just barely.

Then he took her to the small screened porch at the back of the house.

It was one of the first things he'd renovated when he'd moved into the house when Kaine had been a toddler. He'd wanted somewhere safe for her to play that let her be close to the outdoors.

Since no one installed fences in the den, he'd added this porch. For years, it'd been Kaine's playroom. Now it was his.

In the summer, the screened walls kept the bugs out but allowed the sounds and smells of the forest in. The porch ran the entire length of the house so there was enough room for a seating area with a couch, two chairs and a table, and a space big enough for a pool table. He, Aule, Frank and Dorian had spent a lot of nights out there shooting pool and shooting the shit.

No one in the neighboring houses could see into the porch because of the way the houses were situated and he had an uninterrupted view of the woods.

This late, the night was mostly silent except for the crickets, though he faintly heard a few deer and rabbit in the underbrush. He could even hear the faint trickle of the small waterfall in the moon god Tivr's sanctuary not far from here.

One of these nights, he'd take her there.

Tonight, he took her to the comfortable couch along the back wall of the house, so they could look out at the night.

The moon hadn't yet risen but he could feel its pull in his blood. The full moon was only a few days away and though he was long past the time in his life where the moon ruled his wolf, he still felt its call. The *lucani* learned to control their change by the time they hit twenty and Kaisie was way beyond twenty.

Apparently, though, he'd never learned how to control his reaction to a woman he desired more than he wanted his next breath.

He felt as if he was eighteen again and chasing after any woman who'd have him. Which was how he'd gotten Kaine. His kid had been one of the best damn things that'd ever happened in his life so he certainly didn't regret the one night he'd spent with her mother. He just wished Tekeias had let him protect her instead of leaving their child and running off. It'd gotten her killed.

Kaisie learned from his mistakes.

Grace sank into the couch with a sigh, nestling her head into the cushions and staring out at the night. Settling beside her, he sat close enough to feel her body heat but not close enough to touch.

It'd damn near kill him to keep his distance but he needed her to come to him. He couldn't always be chasing after her. He did have some male pride. Okay, he had more than some, which meant he really wanted her to reach for him this time.

Neither of them spoke, though he knew she hadn't fallen asleep.

"He's going to come after them," she finally said. "It's not in his nature to let something he considers his be taken from him."

"If he's not dead already then I'll kill him."

He heard her breath hitch. "It won't be that easy. And…I don't want anything to happen to you."

Now they were making progress. "Are you finally going to admit I'm right?"

"And what do you think you're right about?"

"That you want me and can't live without me."

She didn't contradict him right away and he figured he'd racked up another point in his favor.

When she finally spoke, he wasn't sure if he was going to have to revise that opinion. "Are you planning to kiss me again or are you going to talk me to sleep?"

"Actually," he turned to look at her, "I was kind of waiting for you to kiss me."

Her teeth lodged in her bottom lip and she didn't turn to look at him. "Truthfully, I… I'm not sure I know how. I've never initiated a kiss in my life. I mean, obviously I know the mechanics involved, but there's so much more involved than just mechanics, isn't there?"

He opened his mouth to tell her to just shut up and kiss him already but she moved to lay her head on his shoulder and he snapped his mouth shut.

Yes, they'd had sex but he'd initiated everything up until this point. This was the first time she'd made the move to be close to him.

Now he wanted more.

Greedy? Yeah, and he didn't care.

Then she sighed and he knew he'd lost her focus. "You have to realize I have to take the children and go. He was able to get in here before. Last time, he didn't kill anyone. Next time, he won't be so kind. Ettore is a good *Mal*. He's heartless and ruthless and he'll mow down anyone in his path. I know him, Kaisie. If he's not dead, he's already plotting how to retrieve the children. He found a way in before. He'll find another way in, no matter how you plug the hole."

"I'd rather you go back to talking about kissing."

She sighed, exasperation in the sound. "I don't... You're not... Why me?"

The genuine confusion in her voice hit him below the belt this time. The damn woman had absolutely no idea how desirable he found her. Obviously, he was doing something wrong.

And he didn't know if he could explain it well enough to satisfy her. He'd never been good with words. He was much better at communicating without them.

He wanted to turn to her and take her face in his hands so she could see his eyes when he spoke. He didn't, because he didn't want her to turn away from him. Not now. "You're not afraid to fight with me. You've got a huge fucking heart and you don't take shit from anybody, including me."

After a few seconds, her head lifted and now he turned to see her staring at him, her eyes wide. She didn't say anything though, so he kept going.

"You're smart as hell and you carried my injured daughter to the plane when your arm had to hurt like a sonuvabitch and you were practically bleeding out. You're willing to leave the safety of the den even though you know—"

She cupped his face in her hands and brought her mouth to his, kissing him with a passion that nearly singed his eyebrows.

He didn't see it coming, hadn't thought she'd ever take that first step without a lot more coaxing.

But here she was, kissing him. Her lips molded to his as if learning his taste. And maybe she was. He'd been the aggressor before. He'd consumed her, taken her under and taken her over.

He grabbed the couch cushions and locked himself down, let her explore when he all he wanted to do was strip her naked, lift her over his lap and thrust into her willing body.

A groan rumbled low in his throat as she gained confidence and got bolder with every second. Her mouth moved with more surety, her lips parted and her tongue dipped out to play along the seam of his mouth.

He opened for her immediately but she withdrew and began to press kisses along his jaw. As her hands slid into his hair, twining in the short strands and tightening almost to the point pain, he let his head fall back against the cushion.

She only hesitated a second before straddling his thighs and coming after him.

Her mouth dropped over his again and now he didn't sense any hesitation. She settled her lips against his then slid her tongue into his mouth. Slowly. Feeling her way along. Learning his responses.

He gave them to her freely, let his tongue wind around hers and his cock harden and throb, aching for the feel of her mound rubbing against it. He had his hands cupped around her ass in the next second but resisted the urge to force her down on him.

Instead, he focused on the way she dipped her tongue into his mouth, with delicate, almost tentative strokes that were more arousing than any practiced seduction ever could be. She flicked at his tongue, playing with him, and heat coiled in his gut.

Her fingers tugged on his hair and he answered her silent request by letting his head fall back farther. Her mouth began to press kisses along his jaw and back to his ear, where she nipped the lobe between her teeth.

He shuddered and he felt a smile curve her lips before she nipped his neck just below his ear.

"You make me want to bite you." Her fingers flexed and her breath brushed against his skin, raising his body temperature another ten degrees. "I don't understand what you're doing to me."

"There's nothing to understand. Just don't stop."

Her hips lowered another inch until he thought he could feel the heat radiating from her core.

"The kids—"

"Are out cold and I'll hear them if they wake." He'd make sure he did. "I want you, Grace. And I know you want me. Take me."

She froze for a few dizzying seconds before she sighed. "I don't know what I'm doing."

"Yeah, you do. We did just fine the other night."

"But…what if I want you to take me?"

He cut off his groan at the images her husky question forced into his brain, one of them involving her bent over the side of this couch while he took her from behind.

"Is that really what you want, Grace? Because I'm more than willing to give you exactly what you want."

She pulled back far enough for him to see her eyes, to see the heat and the longing in them.

But it was the uncertain smile that trumped everything. He'd wipe that uncertainty out of her if it took him all night and most of his strength.

"That's what I want."

"Good thing you wore a skirt. Won't have to take it off."

Her eyes widened as she caught his meaning and her pale cheeks flushed bright red. His lips curved in what he made sure was a predatory grin and he took one hand off her ass to cup one of her breasts.

She sucked in a sharp breath as he pinched the hardening nipple between his thumb and forefinger. Her thin green t-shirt and bra did nothing to hide her arousal and the stretchy material of her gray skirt warmed under his hand.

"Come on, babe. Stand up."

"I don't think I'll be able to."

"You won't be on your feet for long, don't worry. Go on. Stand up."

After a second, she eased back so she could use her hands to steady herself as she got to her feet. When she stood looking down at him, he let his gaze drop to her breasts, directly in front of his face. "Take the bra off but leave the shirt."

Her gaze slid to the doors into the house before it locked onto his again and she worked her hands under her shirt and around her back. He saw her bra gape under the shirt then watched as she slid the straps down her arms so she could draw the bra off from beneath the shirt.

Then she dropped it in his lap.

White lace. Damn thing was see-through. He held it up to his nose and sniffed it. His cock throbbed in his jeans. If he wasn't careful, he'd come like a teenager, inside his jeans before he ever got inside her.

"Blessed Goddess, Kaisie…"

He put his hands on her lower thighs, just below the hem of that skirt then he pushed up and under it. The skirt followed, caught on his wrists, until it sat around her waist and exposed the white lace panties that matched the bra.

Filling his hands with the firm, smooth globes of her ass again, he let his fingers dig into the flesh. "Did you wear these for me?"

Her breath audibly caught as his brushed across that soft material. He could smell her arousal, hot and sexy, and he brought his face right up to the vee of her legs. Brushing his nose against the lace, he inhaled.

"I fucking love the way you smell."

Her moan made his hands clench tighter on her ass and he loved the pinch of her fingers when her hands landed on his shoulders to steady herself.

"Hold steady now, because I'm going to taste you."

"Kaisie!"

He smiled at the scandalized tone of her voice. "You're gonna wanna keep your voice down, babe. Don't wanna wake the kids."

He moved in before she could say anything else or squirm away. He pressed a kiss against her mound, right over her clit just before he hooked his thumbs in the sides of those panties and pulled them off her hips.

Her fingers dug into his shoulders as he nuzzled his nose into the trimmed hair on her mound. "Widen your legs, Gracie. There you go. Now hold on."

She stood at the perfect angle for him to get his tongue between her legs and lick at the hardened nub of her clit. With his hands on her ass, he let his tongue part her folds and play with her. Tasting the wetness seeping from her body. She tensed but he didn't wait for her to catch up. If he let her think too much, she'd freeze. He needed to keep her off balance.

And working her into a short, quick orgasm would do just fine to keep her that way.

He didn't tease. He went for flat-out arousal, using his tongue and his teeth and his lips to make her sex clench. Licking at her clit, he played with the tiny nub until it hardened then he stiffened his tongue and slid it between the slick lips of her pussy.

He heard the cry she bit her lips to hold back as he alternately nipped at her clit and fucked her with his tongue. So fucking sweet. The scent of her arousal intensified until finally she came, the muscles of her thighs quivering then tightening as she tried to hold herself steady.

When he stood, she lost the battle not to cry out, clutching at his shoulders as if she thought he was trying to get away.

Instead, he pressed his mouth over hers for a short, hard kiss, knowing she'd taste herself on his lips.

Opening his eyes, he saw the startled, dazed look on her face and it made him growl. He wasn't as careful as he could have been as he spun her around and pushed her over the rolled arm of the couch.

With her skirt still around her waist, he took a moment to stare at her bare ass gleaming in the moonlight. He had the sudden urge to smack that pale skin until it glowed.

Too much, too soon.

Gracie wasn't ready for anything like that.

Hell, just taking her like this was pushing her limits.

Someday soon, though…

"Kaisie…"

Her voice sounded breathless and he loved it. "That's right, sweetheart. Beg me."

She shook he head. "No…"

He stroked his hand across her ass, letting one finger play along the seam and making her squirm. "Oh, yes, you will. You're going to beg me to make you come again."

She gasped, though she tried to hide it. "Do you always talk this much during sex?"

Good thing she couldn't see his expression right now. Didn't want his bared teeth to scare her. "Wouldn't want you to forget who was here with you. Besides, you like to hear my voice."

She gasped as he drew the zipper down on his jeans. "I don't know what to do."

"You don't have to do anything right now. I'm gonna make love to you and the only thing you need to do is enjoy it."

Her hands gripped the cushion until her knuckles turned white. "I want to."

"Then I'll make it good." He let his hands pet her ass and down her thighs then stepped closer and let the tip of his cock brush between her legs. She shuddered and started to push herself up. "No, stay there. Don't move."

He put one hand on the small of her back, the silkiness of her skin distracting him into petting a hand up her spine for several seconds. Until his aching cock drew his attention back to his main purpose.

Getting inside her again. Making her his.

He already knew how hot she'd be, how tight. His heart pounded like a teenager about to get to third base for the first time.

Stroking his hand between her legs, he groaned at the soft, hot flesh spreading around his two fingers. Gods damn, she felt like silk.

Grace moaned, using the cushions to muffle her voice, as he stroked his fingers in and out until she clenched hard around him.

Damn it, she was so close already and he didn't want her to come until he was buried deep inside her.

Slipping his fingers free, he grabbed her hips then held her steady as he positioned his cock. The head brushed against the swollen lips of her sex, making his balls tighten in response to her wet heat.

The sensation was so good, he had to ring the base of his cock with his fingers and squeeze to stave off his orgasm. So fucking good. She felt so fucking good.

He let his cock swipe against that warm flesh, coating him in her wetness and pushing him closer to the edge until he couldn't wait any longer to have her.

With a groan, he thrust forward. Not hard, just enough to bury the head of his shaft between her legs. He stopped so he could soak in the sensation of her snug pussy.

"Oh Gods, Kaisie. That feels..."

Her voice stroked across his senses, and he grabbed tight to his control so he didn't just start to thrust. He needed to make it good for her. Not just get himself off.

"Feel good, baby?" He pushed farther inside, his cock swelling as she gripped him tight. "I want you to feel good."

Her head twisted to the side so he could hear her voice more clearly. "It feels amazing. Don't stop."

His jaw locked as he heeded her command. "I'm not fucking stopping. At least not until you come all over my cock."

Grace gasped and clenched around him, forcing an answering growl from him as he plastered himself against her back and let his hips begin to swing more freely.

Her scent drew him closer and he buried his nose in the softness of her hair at her nape. Damn, she smelled amazing.

He wanted to keep her pinned beneath him all night, keep his dick buried inside her until he couldn't get it up anymore. Which he didn't see happening for hours.

She turned him into a horny teenager all over again. Not that he was complaining.

Especially not when she wriggled her ass against him, telling him without words that she wanted him to go faster. Or clenching around him when she wanted him to go even deeper.

He followed every one of her silent commands, giving her exactly what she wanted.

But it still wasn't enough for him. He wanted to see her face when she came. Wanted to watch her eyes drown in pleasure and her mouth part on each gasp.

When he pulled away, she cried out in frustration, making his lips pull back in a fierce grin.

Pulling her up, he spun her around and slammed his mouth down on hers for a wickedly carnal kiss even as he lifted her into his arms, wrapped her legs around his waist then pressed her back against the arm of the couch and slipped inside her again.

Now he had her exactly where he wanted her. In his arms, plastered against his body. Her arms around his neck, her mouth on his, stealing his breath.

Like two kids in a stolen moment, still dressed and desperate for each other in their parents' living room, they writhed together, straining toward completion.

He felt her hands sink into his hair, clutching and scraping at his scalp. Her legs tightened around his waist, her hips moving in rhythm with his. Her breasts crushed against his chest, tight nipples poking through her shirt. He bent to take one in his mouth. His teeth closed around the tip, causing her to arch and press more of her breast into his mouth.

"Harder. Gods, Kaisie. Harder."

"Yes."

She tried to thrust against him but couldn't get the right angle sitting on the arm of the couch.

So he lifted her, turned and put her back against the wall of the house. Then he loosened his restraint until he lost it all together. His teeth dragged across her nipple until she cried out and yanked on his hair so hard, it hurt.

He licked a wet swath up her throat, tasting salt and sweet, warm woman. Nipping at her jaw, he sucked her skin into his mouth, marking her, as he tunneled into her, his hands filled with her gorgeous ass.

As she clung to him, heels digging into his ass, hands pulling at his hair, he thrust without finesse or control. He covered her mouth with his, kissing her hard, sucking her sweetness into him.

He couldn't get enough of her, strained to get closer, deeper. Emotion boiled in his gut, combining with the lust until he couldn't separate the two.

He needed her with an all-consuming desire. Loved the way she opened only to him.

Her breath felt like a brand against his neck and he let his head tilt back when she opened her mouth on his collarbone to muffle her scream as she came.

She jerked in his arms, her sheath milking his response until he couldn't hold it back anymore and exploded.

Chapter Six

"You're going to be the death of me."

Grace knew immediately that it was absolute wrong thing to say as Kaisie went stone still beside her on the couch.

After they'd come together against the wall and Kaisie had gently cleaned her with his t-shirt, he'd taken her back to the couch on the warm porch and settled her on his lap. With her ear against his chest, she heard his heart calm from thumping arousal to contentment.

"And why do you say that?"

His tone was deceptively calm. In the short time she'd known him, she'd learned that when he sounded like this, he was wary. Full-out pissed involved hand-waving and yelling.

This was worse, she decided.

"I only meant that I can barely breathe when I'm with you. You're like a force of nature, a tornado that's going to spin me around and spit me out. I don't know how to handle you."

He relaxed with a soft huff of a laugh. "Grace, I think you're doing just fine so far. So…when do you want to move in? I should have the new bath and bedrooms framed out by the end of the week. Should be able to call in a few favors, get a few guys over to help. Alex and Amy can share the other bedroom until then. We'll make one of the rooms big enough for Mara and the baby until she figures out if she wants to stay with us or move into her own house. Yours'll be open by then– What? Why are you shaking your head at me?"

Emotions she couldn't control struggled for dominance. Desire, longing, fear. Blessed Goddess, she so wanted exactly what he was offering to her in such nonchalant tones. But she knew she shouldn't. If Ettore was still alive, he'd be coming for her and the children. And he'd kill anyone in his way.

Her hand on his neck gripped him tightly. "How many times do I have to say it, Kaisie? We can't stay here."

"And how many times do I have to tell you everything will be okay? I know trust is hard for you to come by. I understand you're going to have issues that will drive me up a freaking wall. But trust me when I say I'm gonna make it safe for you to stay here."

Her need to kiss him bit at her with sharp little teeth, sinking into her heart. "Short of killing Ettore, you can't ensure that."

She felt him shrug. "Then I'll kill the bastard. No skin off my nose. I can take care of you and the kids. You just have to have a little faith."

Blessed Goddess, she wanted to. And she had no doubt Kaisie could take care of himself. But he was only one man. "I think you may be asking too much of me."

"No, I'm not. You'll see. Everything will work out."

"And when it doesn't? When Ettore descends here with an army and lays waste? What then? I won't be able to live with the knowledge that it's my fault."

"It won't be your fault. It'll be Marrucini's fault. But he won't get the chance because I'll take care of him before that happens."

"Then what about Amy? What are we going to do about her? She's *Mal,* Kaisie. Eventually…"

They'd been over this already. Talking in circles. With a huff, she pushed off his lap and onto her feet. Standing in front of him with her arms on her hips, she wanted to pull her hair out by the handfuls.

But her breasts, still unbound, felt tender and heavy. And her sex still pulsed with remembered sensation, distracting her as she stared down at him.

Kaisie just shrugged. "We'll cross that bridge when we come to it. For now, I don't think we have anything to worry about. She's not going to murder us in our sleep. She hates Ettore as much as you do. No way will she go back to him willingly."

"And if he's still alive then he won't stop until he has her back. And he'll make her pay for what we did."

"Then I'll just have to make sure he can't."

"The only way to make sure is to kill him."

He shrugged again. "Then I'll kill him."

He said it with such calm purpose, she actually shivered, even though it wasn't the first time he'd said it.

She let herself take a few moments to wonder what it'd be like to know Ettore was gone. Completely and forever. She'd planned his death so many times in her mind. She wasn't normally a bloodthirsty person. She was the kind of person who opened a window and shooed out the flies that got trapped in her apartment.

She'd been horrified to learn that the men she'd hired to help her find the right test subjects for her first trials for Alex's drugs had harmed innocents.

Still, it hadn't stopped her from continuing with her experiments, had it?

She'd lived with the specter of Alex's death for so long, the thought of causing anyone's death usually made her physically ill.

Not Ettore's. She would dance on the bastard's grave.

"You would do that for my children?"

"Yes." No hesitation in his voice, his gaze steady. "I'll do it for the kids. Mostly, I'll do it for you."

* * * * *

Kaisie had just set the coffeepot back on its burner when he heard someone knock at the back door. Just once and only loud enough for another *lucani* to hear it.

Cole waited there, wearing a pair of jeans and faded black sweatshirt. Dorian stood at his back in tactical pants and a tight, black top. She reminded him of that actress from the second *Terminator* movie. The one who kicked ass and took names.

"Morning, Kaisie." Cole made no move toward the door when Kaisie opened it.

"Cole, Dorian. You want coffee? Just made a pot."

They both shook their heads but only Cole spoke. "We need to talk. Let's go for a walk."

Well, shit. This wasn't gonna be good. "I'm not leaving them alone."

Dorian rolled her eyes with a barely contained smirk but Cole just nodded. "That's why I came prepared."

Two wolves stalked out of the trees, followed by Race on two feet. Kaisie recognized the wolves as Giovanni and Giorgio Santangelo, two of the most ruthless of the younger soldiers stationed here at the den.

Cole knew Kaisie wouldn't have left Grace and the kids with just anybody. The boy king was good.

And not much of a boy anymore. Kaisie would have to stop thinking of him like that.

"Are we running on two feet or four?" he asked Cole.

"No running. Just a walk and a few words."

Kaisie pushed his feet into the running shoes by the back door, nodded to Race, who nodded back then headed into his kitchen, probably headed straight for coffee. Kaisie thought about waking Grace but she needed the sleep. If she woke before he got back… Well, she'd met Race. So had the kids.

They'd be fine.

They followed the trail back into the woods, the birds making a racket over their nearly silent progress.

No one spoke until they'd gone far enough away from the house that the other soldiers wouldn't hear them.

Finally, Cole paused and leaned against the trunk of a thirty-foot pine.

"All right, spit it out," Kaisie said. "Whatever's—"

"Marrucini's not dead. You need to track him so the *sicarii* can retrieve him."

Fuck. Just…fuck. Even though that's pretty much how he'd thought this was going to go, it still sucked to hear it out loud.

Kaisie sighed and ran a hand through his hair, tugging on the ends to bring his mind into focus. "You're sure."

Dorian sighed, as if disappointed in him, but Cole just nodded. "Yeah. Confirmed by two sources before he disappeared from Florida. We know he's no longer at the same house. We don't think he's left the country but we're not sure. We need to find him and take him alive."

Kaisie's frown made Dorian stand a little straighter at Cole's back. "Alive's going to be a problem."

Cole's brown eyes held steady. "I understand. Doesn't change the facts. We need him alive."

"Why?"

"Because we believe he has information we need. The *Mal* are mobilizing. Have been for a while. You know that. We need him. He's high enough on the food chain. He'll have information we need."

Kaisie wanted to tell Cole to go to hell but he was *Rex*. The *lucani* king. You didn't tell your king to go fuck himself, even if the king was practically still a kid twenty years your junior.

A kid whose parents had been killed by the *Mal* and who'd gotten a crash course in coming into power at the age of seventeen. He'd held on to the crown through sheer force of will and Kaisie admired him all the more for it.

But it didn't change the fact that Kaisie had made a promise.

One he was going to have to break.

"Kaisie." Cole's voice held steady. "I understand why you've got a problem with this. But there're bigger issues here. You *know* that. If I could, I'd give you my blessing to kill the guy. And when we've gotten everything we need from him, I promise, the bastard's yours. But right now, I need you to tell me you can do this."

Reaching for the rational part of his brain that didn't want to rip out Cole's throat, Kaisie took a deep breath and let his head fall back on his shoulders.

The sky above was just starting to lighten with the dawn and he knew he'd have to head back down to Florida to start tracking Marrucini. Leaving Grace and the kids alone.

"I promise you they'll be safe," Cole said as if he'd read his mind. "I'll have Kaine and John move into your place with them until you get back. I'll assign an entire *cohort* to guard them. We've already had the *streghe* replace the wards to ensure he can't get into the den the way he did before."

Fine. It sounded like a great plan.

Grace was gonna think he'd betrayed her. And she wouldn't be wrong. But she'd probably convince herself he'd had to go back on his word. Which he did.

Christ, what a clusterfuck.

The *lucani* had been at war with the *Mal* for centuries, since the *Mal* had briefly enslaved an entire village of *lucani* and forced them to become nothing more than vicious animals to do their bidding.

Cole's great-grandfather had fixed that situation and the world had been lightened of more than a few *Mal* during the bloody liberation.

Now Cole needed leverage. And Kaisie would give it to him.

"I have to tell her."

Cole started to shake his head but Dorian finally spoke up. "Yes, he does. Cole, she deserves to know."

Cole's jaw tightened but he finally nodded after a quick glare at Dorian. "Fine. Tell her he's not dead. Tell her you're going after him. Tell her she won't have to worry about him anymore. Hell, I don't care if you lie and tell her you're going to kill the bastard. Just make sure she knows he's ours."

"We take him alive and the *Mal* are going to declare war."

"That's why we're going to make it look like he's dead."

Which was a hell of a lot tougher than it sounded because the *Mal* would only believe it if they actually had a body in their hands.

"Have we made any progress finding out who's at the head of the *Mal* yet?"

Cole shook his head. "We only know there's been an increase in activity in their businesses. They're making enough money to buy freaking Russia." Frustration had crept into Cole's tone and Kaisie saw weariness in his eyes. "They're up to something and it's not good that we don't have a clue what it is. We need to know. We can't be caught off guard again."

Like Cole's parents and his older brother had been.

Vaffanculo, he needed a drink. "When do we leave?"

*****

Grace opened her eyes and found herself staring at the wall of Kaisie's bedroom.

She didn't remember him carrying her to his bed but he must have at some point.

Catching sight of the clock on the bedside table, she yawned reflexively. Seven a.m. was ungodly early. Especially after last night.

Though she wouldn't give up that memory for anything in the world.

Since Kaisie wasn't in bed with her—and she couldn't decide if she was pissed off about that or not—she figured she'd have to go find him.

Dressed in a t-shirt that was at least two sizes too big, she figured she was covered well enough if the kids happened to see her before she could find her clothes.

Which didn't appear to be in the room.

And she thought she smelled coffee. She would give her right arm for coffee at the moment.

Opening the door to the room slowly, she checked out the living area.

No one around. But the scent of that coffee made her mouth water so she headed for the kitchen.

She found a mug and poured herself a healthy amount. Her eyes closed as the caffeine jolted her system into wakefulness.

After a few minutes of simply enjoying the jolt, she set her now-empty mug on the counter and headed for the other bedroom. The door was already open. She only had to give it a little nudge to allow her to see inside.

Her son and daughter lay back to back on the queen-size bed, sound asleep. They looked more alike in sleep than they did when they were awake.

"They look so peaceful, don't they?"

Grace yelped, unable to help herself as a beautiful blonde stepped toward the bed from the far corner of the room.

Amazingly, the kids didn't stir.

"Oh, don't worry. They can't hear us." The blonde smiled but Grace could see she didn't really mean it. "And don't bother yelling for anyone. No one will hear you. Besides, I'm not going to hurt you."

The beautiful woman didn't look very threatening but Grace couldn't get over the fear that made her heart pound against her ribs.

"Who are you?"

The blonde rolled her eyes and sighed theatrically. "I wondered if you'd recognize me. Guess the *Mal* really are uneducated and unworthy. And here I thought I'd give you the benefit of the doubt."

Through the fog of her fear, Grace realized the woman's face looked familiar. As her brain finally clicked, Grace dropped into a low curtsey. "Lady of the Hammer. My apologies. You startled me and I…I'm so sorry I didn't recognize you right away."

"Well, damn. I guess Lucy's going to have to pay up." Nortia, Etruscan Goddess of Fate, headed for the living room, leaving Grace to follow in her wake. "She was sure you wouldn't know who I was."

"I…I… No, of course, I recognize you, Lady. I just—"

Nortia waved a hand in front of her face, cutting off her apology as if it didn't matter. And it probably didn't. Few deities bothered with the *Mal* anymore. Mostly because the *Mal* didn't bother with them.

"Not here to talk about you, though I'm sure you're an interesting person. We have something else to discuss."

"We do?" With a last glance back at the children, still asleep and oblivious, Grace followed Nortia to the couch, where she'd draped herself elegantly across the center of it.

What could the Goddess of Fate possibly have to discuss with her? Unless she was here to warn her away from Kaisie?

"Wouldn't be here otherwise," Nortia said, and Grace wasn't sure if the goddess was answering her spoken question or her unspoken one.

Grace decided it was in her best interest to shut her mouth and simply listen to what Nortia had to say as she settled onto the edge of the chair across from the couch.

"So," Nortia said, "you want to stay with Kaisie."

"Uh…" Grace's mind went blank.

Nortia raised one sleek, perfect eyebrow. "I need a yes or no. Answer carefully and speak the truth."

The answer was easy enough. She wanted to say yes, which was the absolute truth. But the truth of the matter was so much more complicated. "Lady, I don't… I mean—"

"Grace." The goddess huffed. "There are only two choices here. Choose wisely."

Nortia's blue eyes burned into hers until Grace wanted to run and hide in the bedroom.

Well, fuck that. She was done running.

She didn't want that life for her children. She didn't want it for her.

Taking a deep breath, she sat up and looked straight at the goddess who held the fate of the Etruscans in her hands.

"Yes.

Nortia's smile transformed her face from coldly beautiful to warm and stunning. And when she reached over and patted Grace's hand, Grace felt as if she'd pleased her favorite teacher.

"Good answer. Now the problem, of course, is that your daughter will always be under attack from the *Mal*."

And that was something not even a goddess could change. Amy had been born *Mal*. No one could strip it from her.

"Lady, was that a question? Because if it was, I don't know what answer you're looking to find."

Nortia's mouth curved in a hard smile. "Actually, right now, I'm just laying out the situation. We'll get to the tough part in a minute."

The tough part? Was this where the goddess offered to take the *Mal* curse from her daughter in exchange for Grace's life?

Nortia grimaced as if she'd read her mind. "Yeah, don't look so hopeful. The answer's not as easy as you would hope. Then again, nothing ever is. And you don't know the entire extent of the problem yet."

Okay, now she was totally confused. Her daughter had been born with the *Mal* curse. What could be worse? "Lady Nortia—"

"Yes, yes. I know. You don't understand. And I'm not doing a very good job of explaining, am I?" Nortia sighed, a short harsh exclamation of breath. "There are things about your daughter you're not aware of. Aspects of her…personality that won't be apparent until later in her life. Not even to her."

Okay, that sounded totally ominous. "I don't understand what you're trying to tell me, Lady."

"I know that. And I'm trying not to scare the crap out of you but obviously I'm not doing a very good job."

"Maybe if you just told me—"

"No." Nortia shook her head. "I can't. That information is only for Amalia and only when she's ready. Or I am." Nortia sighed again, sounding disgusted with herself. "Look, Grace, I know this must be totally confusing. I understand your desire to protect your children. I actually admire it and there's not much left in this world that I admire. The problem is…you can't protect Amalia from everything. Amalia's going to have issues to deal with as she gets older. Huge issues that you won't be able to help her with."

The thought made her sick to her stomach. As if a doctor had told her Amy would develop a brain tumor in a few years and there'd be no cure or treatment. "If I can't help her with them, then why are you telling me any of this?"

"Because even though Fate's a bitch, she's not without a heart." Nortia leaned forward and patted her on the knee. "Try not to lose your faith in those around you, Grace. Sometimes there truly is more than one path."

Nortia watched her expectantly, waiting for a response. And since Grace had no idea what to say other than "Okay" that's what she said.

Which seemed to please Nortia, who smiled. "Okay! Wow, I'm so glad we had this little chat. Now I need to go. Kaisie will be back in a minute. Don't be too hard on him. He's only a man, after all."

With the grace of a cat, Nortia rose from the couch and headed out the front door, leaving Grace confused as all hell and wondering if maybe she wasn't still asleep.

Rising from the chair, she walked back into the kitchen to get another shot of caffeine. She'd just taken a sip when Kaisie walked in the door.

His gaze went to her right away, as if he had a sixth sense where she was concerned. Or it could just be her scent.

She let herself stare at him, really look. From his shaggy brown hair that curled at the ends where it covered his nape to the slightly crooked nose. The mouth that made her long for his kiss. That alone was something of a revelation.

Growing up, she'd never fantasized about a fairytale prince coming to sweep her off her feet to a life of romance and happily ever after. She hadn't known that romance novels existed until she'd gone to high school and, even then, she'd only had a vague notion in the back of her mind that there was such a thing.

Her life had been consumed by her parents' demands for the outward appearance of the perfect *Mal* child—demure, quiet, brilliant and obedient. They'd cowed her with threats and punishments. Through fear. Fear of her grandmother, in particular.

Kaisie didn't scare her. He fought with her and pushed her, made her so angry she wanted to scream. And he'd made her crave him.

He held her gaze as he approached. He didn't walk with a swagger, like younger men tended to. He had a natural grace and a confidence that showed through his deceptively laid-back exterior. And even though he seemed to see nothing but her, she knew he'd checked out every square inch of the place.

As he walked over to her, she let her gaze slide down to his broad shoulders and chest. Long and lean, all muscle. Her mouth watered just looking at him. Damn gorgeous man.

He stopped only inches from her, causing her to have to tilt her head back to look up at him. His expression showed nothing but warmth. For her. It put a smile on her lips that he dropped his mouth over and kissed away.

Took her breath away too.

When he pulled back, she knew she had a smile on her face. One he mirrored.

"Good morning." His voice made her want to lick along his throat. "Sorry I wasn't here when you got up. Had to talk to Cole."

His kiss must've scrambled her typical fear response because the mention of the *lucani* king didn't make a blip on her radar.

"What did he want?"

"Work. How'd you sleep?"

"Fine." How would she have slept any way other than fine with him in the same bed? She shivered as he ran one finger along her cheek, wishing she was the type of woman to grab his hand and suck his finger into her mouth. Then she blushed as she realized his mouth had twisted wryly. "Better than fine."

"Glad to hear it." He leaned back against counter, his gaze never leaving hers. "I see you found the coffee."

"Yes. I thought I'd make breakfast, if that's okay."

"Make yourself at home."

"I just didn't want to overstep—"

"Grace." His gaze had the ability to soothe her and fire her up in equal measure. "What part of 'my house is your house' didn't you understand?"

She wanted that. So damn much. She couldn't believe just how much she wanted it.

"So what are you making?"

He had the most beautiful eyes. They made her lose her train of thought. "Making?"

And that smile… "For breakfast?"

She blinked, a flush heating her cheeks. "Oh. I thought I'd make pancakes. Alex loves pancakes."

His eyebrows lifted. "Chocolate chip pancakes?"

"You like chocolate chips?"

He shrugged. "I like anything chocolate. Cover broccoli in chocolate and I'll eat it. I'll drink beer but I prefer rum. I like steak and potatoes and I won't touch asparagus or Brussels sprouts."

Her smile widened and, shutting off the part of her brain that was telling her to move cautiously, she stepped closer to him and let her arms wind around his waist. If she'd surprised him, he didn't show it. Frankly, she'd surprised herself. "Anything else I need to know?"

"Well." He curved his arms around her shoulders and brought her even closer. "I'm an early riser, always have been. I'm pretty good about remembering to close the toilet seat and I usually hang my towel on the bar when I'm done with it. Alex likes me and Amy hasn't shot me yet so I think I'm doing okay there. So, anything you want to tell me?"

What should she say? No one had cared enough to ask her what she liked and didn't like. It made her feel vulnerable. Exposed. But she was no coward. She bit into her bottom lip, worrying it. "Well, I'm kind of a slob, but you probably already figured that out."

He bent down to kiss her, sinking his teeth into her lip for a quick nip. "I won't hold it against you."

"I'm not a very good cook either. I mean, I'd like to be, there's just never enough time and I had to learn most of the basics myself. Growing up, my parents had a cook and so did Ettore. But when Alex and I were alone, I didn't want anyone else in my home, so I had to learn."

"What's your favorite dish?"

She frowned, having to think too hard about the answer to that question. "I don't know." Food had never been high on her list of priorities except for finding things Alex would eat. "Alex likes my pancakes."

"Then you and I'll split the cooking. I'm pretty good in the kitchen. I'm not looking for a maid, Grace."

She shook her head. "What are you looking for?"

"Well, I pretty much think I've been looking for you."

She wanted to melt in a puddle at his feet at the warmth of his tone, the heat in his eyes. Wanted so much to believe she was what he needed. But… "I think you see what you want and not what's really here."

"And I think you've been programmed *not* to see the woman you truly are. The loving mother. The brilliant scientist." He bent and put his lips right up to her ear. "The hot woman who I want to bend over and fuck every opportunity I get. That's what I see."

Her body shook as a wave of desire coursed through her. He'd just described exactly what she wanted to be.

"Kaisie—"

He pressed a kiss to her cheek, sending another shiver through her. "Grace. Why don't you check the cabinets for the ingredients you need for the pancakes. I think I have some mix in there but I'm not sure. You get things started out here and I'll roust the kids. Then…" He sighed. "I'm gonna have to take a trip."

The warmth she'd felt in his arms disappeared as quickly as it'd appeared. She stepped back, out of his arms, and he let her go, shoving his hands in the pockets of his jeans. "He's not dead, is he?"

Kaisie didn't bother to sugarcoat his response but held her gaze steady. "No. We got confirmation this morning. I'll find him, Grace."

She noticed he didn't add anything to the rest of his statement and she didn't know that she wanted to ask what he was going to do when he found him.

He'd promised her he'd kill Ettore. That he'd make it safe for her and the children and Mara.

She didn't want to ask him for his promise again because she didn't want him to tell her he had to break that promise.

So she headed into the kitchen and started searching the cabinets. Behind her, she knew Kaisie watched her for several long seconds before he sighed and headed for the bedroom where the children slept.

This nightmare would never end. Not until Ettore was dead.

Kaisie pushed open the bedroom door, not surprised to see Amy sit up to check out who stood there.

Leaning against the jamb, he let her look around the room, checking all the corners and making sure Alex remained asleep next to her.

When her gaze came back to him, she lost just a little bit of that wariness she constantly wore.

"Good morning, Amy. Sleep well?"

After a brief pause, she nodded but didn't speak.

"Are you hungry? Your mom's making pancakes."

Her head cocked to the side. "Do you think if you keep calling her that, it'll make me believe it?"

He shrugged. "It's true. Just because you don't want to believe it doesn't make it not true."

A look he recognized from Grace covered her daughter's features. "Well, I'm not ready to call her that yet so you need to back off."

"Okay."

It was her turn to look dumbstruck. "Okay? That's all you've got to say?"

Nodding, he moved into the room to stand by the bed, his gaze caught on the crazy pattern of monkeys on her flannel pajamas. She'd seen them in the store and her eyes had lit up though she hadn't reached for them, as if she'd learned not ask for things she truly wanted.

Something else Marrucini would pay for.

But Grace had seen Amy's reaction and she'd casually picked up the bundle and placed it in the cart.

He'd wondered if Amy would wear them. It gave him hope for the future that she had.

"That's all I've got to say. You and your mom are gonna have to work this out on your own. I just want you to give her the opportunity to become your mom. She had no chance before. Okay? That's all I'm asking. And since I'm not going to be around for a couple of days, I need to make sure you understand how important it's going to be for you to be on your toes."

He thought he saw genuine distress flash through her eyes. "Where are you going?"

"I've got to take a trip. Work."

Her eyes narrowed and she let her gaze fall to Alex, still asleep on the other side of the queen-size bed, before she trained those dark eyes on him again. "He's not dead, is he?"

Kaisie refrained from shaking his head but, damn, when had he lost the ability to hide anything? Still, he wasn't going to lie to the girl. "No. But like I promised your mom," and, he used the word "promised" deliberately, "I'll find him and I'll take care of him."

Her mouth set in a flat line. "Will you kill him?"

"I can't. At least not right away. The *lucani* need to talk to him, find out what he knows. He may have information that could help us."

"Is that why you took me? For information?"

Again, that hurt in her eyes, the emotion she tried to keep hidden. She looked exactly like Grace at the moment and it tore at his heart.

"No, Amy. I took you because I made a promise to your mom. She wanted to find you. She was willing to give her life in exchange for you and Alex. You need to keep that in mind when you're telling yourself she's not really your mom."

He let the girl think about that for a moment before he reached out to ruffle her hair. She froze but didn't move away as his hand brushed over her soft, dark hair.

He had a feeling the girl had no idea how to accept affection. That she hadn't been hugged or kissed like a normal kid. Like her mother. But her mother had learned and so would Amy.

"Now it's time to get up. We'll have breakfast. Then I'm going to leave and make sure you and Alex and your mom don't have anything to fear from Ettore Marrucini ever again."

Chapter Seven

Grace flipped pancakes onto a plate, surprised she hadn't burned the damn things.

Her mind definitely hadn't been on the task at hand.

Instead, she'd been thinking. Which wasn't a stretch for her. Her mind never really stopped working. But this wasn't about science or curing her son.

This was about freeing her children. About freeing herself from the clutches of the *Mal*.

The logistics would take some finessing. And she thought Kaisie might have a fit.

But if she could get Cole in her corner on this one, Kaisie wouldn't have much of a defense.

Especially if her plan got Cole one step closer to the head of the *Mal*. She didn't know who that was. But she knew someone who should.

But it meant she'd have to head into the lion's den.

She needed to talk to her grandmother.

Just the thought was enough to make her stomach twist and pitch.

But if Cole agreed to her plan, she might be able to buy her children out from the noose of the *Mal*.

Of course, her grandmother might kill her in the process but there was a certain amount of risk in every plan.

She was willing to take this one.

Behind her she heard footsteps and the wonderful dull thump of Alex's crutches. Her eyes teared up every time she heard them. Blinking them back, she turned with a smile and the plate of pancakes and almost lost it completely.

She'd never let herself hope for this moment, when her daughter and her son would be sitting down to breakfast at the same table. And she'd never let herself imagine a man like Kaisie looking at her the way he was now.

She wanted to keep this moment, right now. Hold on to it with both hands and fight for it.

Kaisie had to understand that. She'd have to make him understand.

But first she had to beat her grandmother at her own game.

She managed to get through breakfast without making too much of a mess of things.

Amy actually spoke to her. Two whole sentences consisting of "How's your arm?" and "I slept fine. Thanks."

But she said them without a hint of sneer and that made it all worthwhile. She talked to Kaisie more and had a few smiles for her brother.

But that wariness never left her eyes.

And hardened Grace's resolve.

"Hey, guys," Kaisie said, after all the pancakes had been consumed. "Do me a favor and put the dishes in the dishwasher. I need take your mom somewhere. We'll be back in about a half-hour."

"You're leaving us here alone?"

Alex's brief flash of fear made him blush as he stole a look at Amy but Kaisie gave him an easy smile. "Only for a few minutes. You know, I think Kaine's outside with John on patrol. Bet she'd love to come in and watch a few cartoons with you."

Of course that placated Alex and even Amy seemed okay with it.

A few minutes later, Kaisie and Grace walked through the woods on a path Grace had never seen before.

"Where are we going?"

"I've got to leave soon but I wanted to show you something before I go."

They walked in silence for a few more seconds.

Then she couldn't help herself. "How long will you be gone?"

"I should be back by tomorrow morning. Don't worry. I'll be back soon."

Hopefully not too soon. At least not before she'd gotten Cole to agree to her plan and put it into play. Kaisie would pitch a royal fit if he knew what she was going to do.

Pushing all that aside for the moment, she let herself enjoy the walk with him, her hand in his. Even though the temperature hovered in the mid-forties, she didn't feel cold in jeans, a t-shirt and a fleece sweatshirt. Kaisie wore even less, only black pants and a gray long-sleeved t-shirt. She swore the man had a little bear in his background. She didn't think he felt the cold at all.

After a few minutes, she heard the sound of running water and when Kaisie stopped, she continued on into the clearing ahead of him.

Her breath caught at the simple beauty of the spot, the waterfall bubbling from the outcropping of rocks, the carpet of moss in front of the waterfall, still green despite it being winter. Which it didn't feel like here.

As she stepped farther into the clearing, she swore the temperature rose at least ten degrees, making her almost too warm.

"This is Tivr's sanctuary," Kaisie said.

"It's beautiful."

"Yeah, Ty knows how to decorate."

She walked over to the falls, let her hand play in the water. Metallic glints beneath the surface caught her eye, like tiny, trapped stars.

She felt Kaisie move behind her then felt his arms wrap around her waist from behind. His hips pressed against her ass, his erection hard and hot.

He didn't grind against her, didn't do anything except hold her. But each second in his arms, held against the length of his strong body, she felt her blood heat.

She knew why he'd brought her here. Knew he wanted to make love to her here, in this place that felt sacred.

She wanted the same but needed him to hold her, just for a few minutes. And he seemed content to do it.

Resting her head back against his chest, she closed her eyes, her hands stroking along his forearms.

Until it wasn't enough. She needed more.

She turned in his arms, circling hers around his shoulders and lifting her mouth to his.

The second his lips touched hers, she felt that spark ignite low in her body and gave herself over to it.

She wanted their clothes to disappear so she could crawl up his body and wrap herself around him. Wanted him to sink inside her and make her forget everything for just a few minutes.

As if he'd read her mind, his fingers slipped the button on her jeans then worked the zipper down. He had her pants halfway down her legs by the time she unbuckled his belt.

And she gasped when he spun her around, stretched her arms out to steady herself against the nearest tree trunk and ran one warm hand across her bare ass. Shuddering at the flare of heat that stole her breath and made her sex clench in anticipation, she braced herself and spread her legs as far apart as she could with her pants around her ankles.

She had a momentary image of how they looked, half-dressed and panting, Kaisie's hand brushing against her ass as he shoved his jeans down far enough to release his erection.

Then he moved in, letting that hot flesh slide between her legs and rub against her slick sex.

"Kaisie."

He brushed the hair from her nape and pressed his lips against the sensitive skin there, making her shiver.

"Kaisie, I—"

"Unless you're about to say, 'Kaisie, I want you to do me,' I don't want to hear it."

She arched back against him, rubbing herself against his cock and making him draw in a sharp breath. "Kaisie, I do want you to do me. And…"

He began to thrust between her legs, the tip of his cock hitting her clit and sending her closer to orgasm with every pass. "And what?"

Rational thought escaped her as he angled his cock a little differently and the head slipped into her body. She gasped at the rush of heat that flooded her sex and spread outward then nearly cried when he retreated.

"And what, Grace?"

She let her head hang as she tried to collect her thoughts and found she couldn't. "And I think I'm falling in love you."

His groan was music to her ears. "Ah, Grace, you just think you're falling in love with me? Damn, I already know I love you."

With a shift of his hips, he sank deep.

Her heart stuttered at the words she'd honestly never thought to hear from a man. Emotion drenched her in heat and she grabbed his forearms to anchor him to her.

She thought he would start a hard and fast rhythm but he surprised her by taking it slow and steady. Making her feel every drag and push against sensitive internal tissue.

His arms held her tight, his lips pressing kisses against her neck.

Blessed Goddess, she felt loved. She'd never felt anything like it. It made her blood burn. It wasn't sex. She'd had sex before. She'd never made love.

She liked this a whole hell of a lot better.

Turning her head, she sought his mouth. As if he knew what she wanted—and maybe he did—he turned his head to meet her lips.

His kiss took her breath, made her burn and pushed her closer to that edge.

Kaisie must have felt the same as he started to thrust faster.

Because she wanted this feeling to last, she tried to hold on to it without tipping over that edge.

But Kaisie wouldn't allow it. He slid one hand between her legs to stroke her clit. She only needed one caress to push her past that point and she cried out as she came.

Kaisie went with her, somehow managing to hold both of them upright.

"Say it again." His voice, husky, practically a growl, made her sex clench around him harder. "Without the unnecessary words."

She knew what he wanted her to say and she gave up any pretense of indecision.

"I love you."

"Damn right you do."

She wanted to laugh at the arrogance in his tone but couldn't muster the strength. The man simply slayed her.

And she loved it. She loved him.

They were going to need all the luck in the world to make this work.

* * * * *

"So, either Seth or Race will be here at all times, as well as another set of guards, who'll rotate every couple of hours. You might not see them but don't worry. They're out there."

Grace nodded at John, sitting with her on Kaisie's couch, while Kaine shared a peanut butter and jelly sandwich with Alex at the table. Alex had developed a serious crush on Kaisie's daughter, and Kaine appeared to return the affection.

She joked with Alex, talked to him as if he was a person and not a kid. Not an invalid. Kaine even tried to draw Amy into the conversation, though Amy didn't have more than monosyllabic answers to anything Kaine said.

Grace couldn't say as she blamed her daughter. Since Kaisie had left this morning, none of them had been in the mood for much of anything. All she could do was worry, though she tried not to show it in front of the kids.

They had enough of their own anxiety. They didn't need to see hers.

So, accompanied by Seth and Race, Grace had suggested they all go visit Mara in the medical center, where Grace made her first halting attempts to speak to the frightened teenager.

At least Mara had seemed more friendly to Grace than Amy so Grace took that as a good sign. She'd told the girl not to worry about anything. That she and the baby would be well taken care of and would have everything she needed.

Grace didn't blame the girl for looking skeptical. It'd take some time. But Grace felt a kinship with Mara that she hoped would see them through the rough time ahead. Hell, it was going to be a rough time for all of them.

When they'd returned to Kaisie's house, Grace had discovered someone had moved all of their clothing from the other house.

Hers was in Kaisie's bedroom, stacked neatly on his bed. The kids' were in the other room, most of it already hung in the closet or put in the dressers.

And Kaine and John had been sitting at the dining room table.

Amy had stilled like a doe in the headlights before she'd slunk off to the bedroom without a word.

Kaine had flashed Grace an apologetic smile before she'd engaged Alex in a conversation about some book they'd both apparently read. How Kaine knew that, Grace had no idea. But Alex had a smile on his face and that was all that mattered.

"Grace?"

With a start, Grace refocused her attention on John. Kaine's handsome, ex-Navy SEAL mate had a piercing stare that made her feel as if he could read her mind. She still had a hard time looking him in the eyes after what she'd done to him and his sister.

She'd kidnapped him and kept him in a cell while she tested his blood. He'd been rescued by the *lucani* before the men she'd hired to help her had been able to hurt him. She'd never wanted to hurt anyone. She'd only wanted to save Alex.

"I don't think I'll ever be able to apologize enough for what I did to you, John."

His gaze narrowed for a brief second before he settled a little deeper into his chair. "And I've told you before, I'm fine. Evie's fine. And Alex is still alive. We move on from there, Grace."

"And wouldn't it be wonderful if it was just that easy."

"Nothing's ever easy. But you've got to learn to let your past go before it fucks up your future."

She let her gaze slide toward Alex for a brief second, to make sure he was engaged by Kaine. "I'd like to think I have a future. But…I'm no naïve teenager. Actually, I never was. And I know there are going to be people here who will never accept me."

"But there's one very important man who does." John held on to her gaze when she would have dropped his. "Do you really want to let him down?"

"No, of course not. I actually had a dream last night about being happy. Here. With Kaisie."

"Then that's what you need to focus on."

She was trying. Still… "My children and I will never be free as long as Ettore's breathing. I understand why your king might want him alive but you can appreciate my dilemma."

He nodded, his eyes narrowing. "I can."

She took a deep breath, knowing he was her only hope to implement the plan that'd been formulating. "And can you tell me how I should deal with the terror of knowing my children will never be safe? That Mara and her baby will always be looking over their shoulders, trying to stay one step ahead?"

"You know I can't."

"I may know someone who can bring Ettore to heel. Someone who has the power to take care of Ettore forever." She took a deep breath and prepared to ask probably the hardest question she'd ever asked. "Will you help me, John?"

His gaze narrowed. "Help you how?"

"Will you take me to see someone who may be able to help me fix this mess with Ettore and get the *Mal* off our backs?"

*****

"What do you mean she's gone?"

"She and John and two *praetorians* left an hour ago," Kaine said. "I promised I'd give them a head start before I called you. I think it's been long enough."

Kaisie swore until he figured the phone lines had blistered. He and Duke and Nic were waiting at a private airfield outside Tampa for the chartered plane to be refueled so they could follow Marrucini to New York City.

Kaisie had picked up the bastard's scent not far from the house, just the faintest trace but enough for Kaisie to follow. At first, he'd thought the bastard had been playing with him, laying down a false trail. But the longer they followed, the more he became convinced that the man was injured pretty badly and not in any shape to be screwing with them.

"Where were they headed?"

"New York City. She's going to talk to her grandmother."

"What? Why the hell would she do that?"

"Grace said she can get her grandmother to rein in Marrucini somehow."

Son-of-a-fucking-bitch.

"Get in touch with John." He motioned for Nic to come closer. "Tell him Marrucini's on his way to New York and he can't take Grace anywhere near the *Mal*."

"Shi—"

The phone clicked in his ear as Kaine hung up.

Shit was right. "Duke. We gotta go now."

Duke's dark eyes narrowed and he stood. The guy did nothing fast but at least he was moving. "What's up? Marrucini—"

"Is in New York and so is Grace. I don't want him anywhere near her."

Duke's eyebrows lifted. "She went alone?"

"John's with her and two *praetorian* guards."

Duke visibly relaxed. "He knows what he's doing. She's in good hands."

"I know that but I need to be there with her."

Duke shrugged. "So you'll be there."

Kaisie felt his anxiety levels rise as Duke didn't seem to see the seriousness of the situation. "I'm gonna call John and tell him to stall. Tell the pilot to get us in the air as soon as possible and fly us straight to NY."

Duke's raised eyebrow made those levels skyrocket. "Damn, Kaisie. Maybe you need to have a drink and chill out."

Okay. Duke was a dead man.

Kaisie shot out with a right hook before he even realized he'd done it. And when he connected with Duke's chin, he immediately realized Duke had let him land that punch.

"Feel better?" Nic asked from somewhere behind him. "I know I always feel better after I hit Duke."

As Kaisie shook out his throbbing fist—damn Duke's fucking rock-hard chin—he shot Duke the finger with the other then turned to Nic.

"We better be fucking ready to take off."

Nic's smile spread. "Yeah, we're ready. Course correction already logged."

"How the hell did you— She called you first, didn't she?" Damn, he loved his daughter but they'd be having a very frank conversation when he and Grace got back to the den.

"Yeah, she did, but only because she knew you'd want to be in the air as soon as possible and she knew I'd get it done fast."

Kaisie looked at first Duke then Nic. They knew how he felt about Grace. They didn't have to ask and he didn't have to say anything. They had a mate they loved. Who they'd die for, if it came to that.

He sighed as he started toward the plane. "I reserve the right to kick your asses at a later date."

Duke actually smiled. "Must be getting weak in your old age, man."

"I can still take you down, Duke. Don't piss me off."

Nic started to cough though Kaisie knew the bastard was laughing at him. "I'm cutting you some slack since you actually did something useful and got the plane in the air faster. But don't push it."

"She'll be fine, man." Duke caught up to him just inside the cabin on the eight-passenger jet. "Don't get yourself worked up about a situation that may never happen. It won't help."

As Kaisie buckled himself in, Duke and Nic did the same across the aisle and the pilot started the engine.

He knew what Duke was saying but that didn't help ease the sick lump in the pit of his stomach.

* * * * *

Grace hadn't seen her grandmother in a year and a half, at least.

And she hadn't missed the woman, she thought as John drove through the Lincoln Tunnel.

Graziella Bellasario would rather ruin or destroy your reputation and career than bake cookies on a lazy Sunday afternoon.

Graziella ran a successful, diversified company, parts of which spread throughout the United States and Italy. Her husband had died shortly after the birth of their son. Car accident.

Grace didn't think it'd been much of an accident. There were no accidents around her grandmother. Everything went according to plan. Her plan.

The only thing that hadn't was Grace being born without a caul. And Graziella had never let Grace forget it.

As a child, Grace had been terrified of her grandmother. Her cold eyes, her too-calm voice, her expressionless face. Frankly, the woman creeped her out.

Graziella had that effect on a lot of people. Business rivals had been known to call her the Serpent Woman behind her back. Grace thought her grandmother secretly liked it because no one who'd ever used the nickname had turned up missing.

The same couldn't be said about business associates who failed her. Some of them were never seen again.

Grace knew her grandmother wouldn't hesitate to get rid of her own flesh and blood if she disappointed her. Especially since she'd already done her duty and produced a *Mal* heir to a respected *Mal* family.

She was expendable. At least, that's what her grandmother had considered her.

But she didn't know Grace. She'd never taken the time to get to know her. Graziella had always considered her a pawn without much of a brain for business.

Well, Grace had learned.

She just hoped she'd learned enough to bargain with her grandmother so she, John and the two *lucani* following them in another car would walk out of Graziella's office with their hearts still beating.

The woman may be closing in on ninety but her power had strengthened instead of waned over the years.

Doubt wanted to derail her.

Why had she ever thought this would work?

And why had Cole agreed to let her try? Maybe he'd known she would fail and her grandmother would kill her and he wouldn't have to worry about her anymore.

He couldn't honestly believe she'd have any hope in hell of making this work.

Then again, why would he have sent John and two other *lucani* to keep her safe?

No time to second-guess herself now as John made his way through the madness of Midtown traffic to get to Sixth Avenue.

She directed him to a parking garage not far from her grandmother's building, followed closely by Cole's *praetorians*. They parked then made their way back to street level.

Turning automatically toward her grandmother's building, she started to walk until John laid a hand on her arm as he put his phone to his ear.

"Hey, Kaine, what's—"

He fell silent, his eyes narrowing and she knew whatever Kaine was telling him, it wasn't good.

"The kids?" she forced herself to ask as the *praetorians* stopped at her back.

John shook his head and her chest loosened the slightest bit. "Kaisie?"

John held up his index finger and she nearly had to bite her tongue off to stay quiet.

After at least a minute of one-sided conversation on the other end of the phone, John said, "Okay," and hung up.

"Kaisie will be here in half an hour. We wait for him before we do anything."

Her mouth hung open for a second before she got her brain to work. "What? Why?"

John put his arm around her shoulders and started walking again, as if they were a couple out of a stroll. "He's pretty sure Marrucini's here in the city. Kaisie thinks Marrucini's damaged pretty badly."

"And he thinks Ettore has gone to my grandmother for help?" She shook her head. "No. No way. My grandmother would tell him to clean up his own mess. She'd think him weak if he came to her for help."

"Then it won't matter if we just hang out for a while and wait for Kaisie."

She wanted to stomp her foot and insist that John take her immediately to her grandmother's. She wanted to get this over with now.

"And when Kaisie gets here, he's going to demand that I go back to the den without talking to her. No, we have to do this before he gets here. Cole okayed this, John. He believes I have a shot. Kaisie will want to hustle me back to the den and hide me away. I believe he means well but—"

"You don't know that. The man loves you, Grace, whether he's said the words or not. He's worried about you. He doesn't want anything to happen to you."

"I understand that. I do. But I'm not a soldier. I don't take orders. I'm old enough to make my own decisions and I have you and two highly trained soldiers at my back. If Kaisie's here…" She paused and released a heavy sigh. "If he's here, I may listen to him. I may tuck my tail between my legs and run home. I'm sick of running."

John stared down at her, his expression torn but resigned.

"You know Kaisie will have my ass for this," he finally said.

She shook her head, trying to look much more confident than she felt and probably failing miserably. "No, he won't because this will be over before he can do anything about it. And everything will be fine."

And it would have been. If only her grandmother hadn't been a little too sure of herself.

Grace walked into her grandmother's building as if she owned it. Which wasn't far from the truth. She was Graziella's only grandchild. One day, she would own it.

Of course, after today, her grandmother would probably disown her, so…

Stepping up to the reception desk just inside the doors, she stared directly at the receptionist. "I'm here to see Graziella Bellasario. Please tell her personal secretary Grace Bellasario is here."

The young woman's expression changed from haughty to wide-eyed in two seconds flat as she reached for the keyboard. "It will only take me a second, Ms. Bellasario. Why don't you have a seat while you—"

"I don't expect to be kept waiting long enough to need a seat."

The receptionist's eyes got even wider. "I'll just—" She pressed a few buttons then spoke into the slim microphone attached to the earpiece. "Ms. Conacelli? Grace Bellasario is here to see Mrs. Bellasario. Should I— Yes. Of course. Of course."

The young woman turned back to Grace with a trembling smile. "Please take elevator five to the top floor. I'm afraid your men—"

"Will be coming with me." Grace smiled at the girl, who couldn't be much older than twenty-three or -four. She'd been told, though she'd never really seen the resemblance before, that she looked like her grandmother. When the girl's smile died and actual fear made her blanch, Grace figured the resemblance had only gotten stronger with age.

At least her grandmother didn't look like the Wicked Witch of the West.

As Grace turned toward the bank of elevators beyond the reception desk, John and the two *praetorian* guards followed. They played the role of bodyguards perfectly, staying a few steps behind her and not talking to her.

The guard at the elevators pressed the button for her, never making eye contact.

Grace sensed no magic at all from the man and had a brief second to wonder at that before the mirrored doors opened.

John stepped around her to check out the interior of the elevator before he nodded at her, and she and her other two guards entered.

The ride up was silent, though she exchanged a meaningful glance with John.

That'd been too easy.

Her grandmother never would have allowed Grace to bring three unknown men with her into Graziella's inner sanctum.

Which meant they were either heading into a trap or her grandmother didn't think Grace represented any kind of threat.

True, John had no magic at all but the *praetorians* reeked of it. They were powerful *lucani*.

When the elevator dinged to mark their destination, Grace knew something was horribly wrong.

Which proved to be true when the doors slid open and Ettore Marrucini stood there.

"Hello, Grace. Nice of you to join us."

* * * * *

Kaisie had never much cared for cities but he'd spent a lot more time in them than either Duke or Nic had.

He knew the fastest way to get to where they were going from Newark, where their plane had landed. He knew where to park the car and how to navigate the midmorning crowds on Sixth Avenue.

Duke and Nic kept up with him only because they knew if they lost him, Cole and Kaine would have their asses. But he wasn't about to make allowances for them.

Not when Grace was in danger.

By the time he pushed through the doors of the Bell building, he knew Marrucini was already there, as was Grace, and he was in no mood to tap dance with the receptionist who looked as if she'd just stepped off a photo shoot for a fashion magazine.

"Send me where you sent Grace Bellasario. Right now."

The girl, who looked younger than his daughter, barely blinked as she fake-smiled at him. "I'm sorry, sir. Do you have an appointment?"

Her expression changed fast enough when he growled at her. "No, I don't. And I don't need one because you really don't want to mess with me right now, little girl. There's an injured, possibly unbalanced *Mal* with low impulse control on the loose in your building and, if you don't open the damn elevator and let us go find him, my associates and I are going to change into wolves right here and tear through the guards and anyone else who tries to get in my way. Do you understand?"

Any other day, he would've handled this situation much differently. But on any other day, his mate would *not* have deliberately placed herself at risk by leaving the den to speak to her *Mal* grandmother and leaving herself open to an attack by her crazy ex.

Behind him, Duke motioned to Nic, who turned to face the guards who'd seemingly appeared out of nowhere. Two of them had low-level power, the third, strictly human.

Kaisie never took his eyes off the receptionist. "I am not here to hurt you. I'm not here to hurt anyone except Ettore Marrucini. But if you don't—"

"Shit, Kaisie. I think we're gonna be late to the party."

All of the guards started to run for the elevators and Kaisie motioned for Duke and Nic to follow them. Then he nodded to the young receptionist. "You're going to want to leave. Now. I'd suggest you get out and don't come back. Trust me, you'll find a better job elsewhere. One that won't involve crazy people and werewolves."

Her eyes widened as he took off at a run to the elevators, where Duke and Nic had already convinced the guards to let them go with them to where they were going in such a hurry.

Of course, the boys hadn't given them much choice in the matter, as Nic had shifted into his pelt and growled at them and Duke had swiped one of their weapons.

Kaisie looked at the gun then at Duke, who shrugged.

"What? I can't play with their toys?"

"Don't hurt yourself with it or Tira will have my head."

Nic snorted, shaking his head and twitching his tail back and forth. One of the guards actually tried to take another step back but couldn't because he'd come up against the wall.

"Hey, man," Kaisie said, "if the wolf freaks you out, you might want to make a run for the doors because that's nothing compared to what you're gonna see on the top floor."

The guy did exactly what Kaisie told him to do and Duke turned to watch him run before he turned back to Kaisie with one lifted eyebrow. "Dude, you've got such a way with words."

Kaisie gave him the finger. "Anybody else wanna make a break, now's the time."

The two guards who remained held their ground, never turning their backs, not even to get on the elevator.

The ride up was quiet except for the tasteful classical music pumped in through the speakers. It drove him fucking insane while he watched the numbers count upward and Duke and Nic kept an eye on the guards.

"Kaisie, she'll be fine. John's with her. He won't let anything happen to her."

He knew that. He knew his daughter's mate would take a bullet for Grace. And wouldn't that be fucking awful. To have to tell his daughter John had been killed defending Kaisie's mate.

Fucking hell.

He shoved that thought out of his mind. He needed to have his head on straight or he'd be the one they dragged out in a body bag.

By the time the doors opened, he'd managed to get his game face plastered on, despite the fact he'd been able to smell blood since he'd gotten in this little metal box.

And when the elevator opened into an office that looked like a warzone, he had to mentally hogtie his wolf to stay calm.

Two large men lay on the floor outside the elevator. They accounted for some of the blood he smelled. But not all.

Kaisie stared into the spacious reception area that guarded a single door behind it. That door stood open and Kaisie could smell the scent of blood coming from there. As well as Grace's and John's scents.

He saw no one else but could now make out the voices he'd been able to hear but not understand before. Grace, angry, haughty. Another, older woman he didn't recognize but who had the same haughty attitude as Grace. Then John, low and timid, speaking to Grace, trying to get her to be quiet, to calm down.

John was working an angle. Unfortunately, Kaisie didn't know enough about the situation to know what angle. He could fuck up John's plan if he walked into that room without knowing what the hell was going on.

Yet, he couldn't wait out here any longer.

He motioned to Duke and Nic, letting them know he was going in and they were to wait outside the room for his signal. Duke rolled his eyes and Nic bared his teeth and shook his head but Kaisie had too much to lose in this scenario and he wasn't about to trust anyone else with Grace's and John's lives.

Slipping out of the elevator, he headed toward that open door.

"Ettore, stop this madness right now." The older woman, who Kaisie assumed was Grace's grandmother, snapped out words with the attitude of someone who expected to be obeyed. "You will not murder my granddaughter. She's offered to go with you to retrieve the children. What more do you want?"

"What you promised me, old woman. This company. Grace did her part. I don't give a shit about her. I want my daughter and I want what you told me was mine when I agreed to let Grace and Alex go that first time. But you backed out of the deal, you bitch. So I took back the boy."

"But you couldn't keep him, could you? Or my daughter."

That was Grace again, deliberately goading Marrucini as Kaisie's blood froze. He hoped like hell she knew what she was doing, that she knew, somehow, that he was here. Because if she didn't…

Kaisie had made it to the door without being seen but he still hadn't been gotten a look inside the room. The door was only open a few inches.

So he got on his stomach and crawled the rest of the way. He thought about shifting into his wolf but figured Marrucini would be able to sense the magic when he did and he didn't want to give the guy any reason to suspect anything.

Obviously, he hadn't sensed their arrival or he would've sent someone out here to check them out. Kaisie couldn't believe the guy had come alone. Especially since he was injured.

Taking a deep breath, he scented the acrid odor of Marrucini's pain, Grace's fear and anger, another female's fury, John's cold calculation...and now he picked up on the scents of two other men in the room. They were faint but there. Almost completely blocked, even from his senses.

Shit. Guess he was going to have to do this the hard way.

Motioning for Nic to come at the door from the other side of the room, he slid forward, trying to get a peek into the room without actually sticking his head into the doorway.

He got lucky. The floor-to-ceiling tinted windows provided a hazy picture of part of the room.

John stood just inside the door. That was good. The two goons holding guns on him, not so good.

An older woman he was assuming was Grace's grandmother stood to the left of him with another goon on her. Again, not so good. But Kaisie didn't give a shit if Grace's grandmother got caught in the crossfire. That bitch would deserve whatever she got.

He couldn't see Marrucini or Grace so he had to assume they stood to the right of the door.

The back and forth between Marrucini, Grace and her grandmother continued, but Kaisie barely listened to the words. His brain was running strategy, his anxiety increasing as he picked up on the escalating threat in Marrucini's tone.

He wanted to warn John but couldn't see a way. John was smart and fast and he'd figure it out.

Looked like the only options they had were speed and surprise.

He signaled to Nic, who nodded, then turned to do the same to Duke.

Kaisie's mouth curved in a grin. Duke had been busy. He'd knocked out the guards from the elevator and used their unconscious bodies to hold open those doors. They didn't need to be looking over their shoulders while they got Grace and John out of there.

Okay. Time to go get his woman.

*****

Grace felt Ettore shaking behind her.

The arm he held around her neck practically cut off her air supply but she forced herself not to struggle.

She and her grandmother had been tag-teaming Ettore for the past ten minutes, trying to buy time. Goading him.

Kaisie was on his way. She just had to hold out until Kaisie got here.

Not that she planned to play the damsel in distress. No, she was going to kill Ettore herself. She just needed Kaisie to distract the bastard so she could take the knife he held at her side and jam it down his throat.

It would end his life too quickly but that couldn't be helped.

The bastard had planned to sell their daughter to the highest bidder after her grandmother had handed him her business.

She couldn't believe her grandmother had planned to give the business to Ettore. Grace wondered if her father knew. Not that she really cared but, damn, her father would be crushed. Which she figured didn't come close to being what he deserved.

"I want you to sign the papers now, Graziella. Sign everything over to me and I'll allow your granddaughter to live. She and the children will live with me. We'll all be so happy in New York, won't we, Grace?"

"But you'll never find the children, Ettore. Trust me, they're far from your control now."

Blessed Goddess, she could practically smell the rage coming off him. And the stink of injury. He was hurt badly. His skin burned against hers and he was drenched in sweat.

Unfortunately, he could still stand and hold a knife to her chest.

She choked a little as his arm tightened and she saw John's eyes narrow with deadly intent. He was going to get himself killed defending her. And that was simply unacceptable.

She stared at John, tried to get him to relax, but he had his gaze laser-sighted on Ettore.

Blessed Goddess, please, she silently prayed as her grandmother spoke in haughty tones about betrayal and consequences and Ettore raged back. Their words meant nothing to her. *Please don't let John be hurt. Kaine would be inconsolable.*

Because she was watching him so closely, she saw John's attention waver for a brief second. His gaze focused on a point just over Ettore's shoulder. Something in the window.

Ettore's focus never wavered from her grandmother. The guards made no movement.

Then John's gaze shifted back to her and he mouthed one word. She hoped like hell she got it right because, out of the corner of her eye, she caught a flash of movement.

Closing her eyes, she forced her body to go limp as all hell broke loose.

Ettore let her drop as the growls of two wolves echoed in the room. Shouting and gunfire erupted around her and her first thought was to find Kaisie. She knew he was here.

Above her, Ettore howled with rage and she opened her eyes to see a fast-moving blur jump at him. With a startled cry, she scrambled out of the way as Kaisie took Ettore to the ground.

The knife Ettore had been holding fell out of his hand and she lunged for it, grabbing it and moving as far away from the men as she could.

She had no doubt that Kaisie would best Ettore but she wasn't going to give Ettore any advantages.

When she reached the wall of windows, she stood, holding the knife out in front of her. Beside her, she felt her grandmother stand next to her.

She kept her eyes on Kaisie, ready to fight beside him if he needed her, which it didn't appear that he did. Ettore was fighting for his life and he knew it but Kaisie was wearing him down.

"I'm assuming you know these men?"

Her grandmother's quiet comment drew Grace's attention away from the fight for a brief moment.

"Yes."

"That one." She pointed at Kaisie, currently pounding his fist into Ettore's face. "He's claimed you."

Grace wanted to laugh at the archaic phrasing but considering it was basically true, she didn't bother to contradict her grandmother.

"Yes."

Grace winced as Ettore landed a blow, drawing blood from Kaisie's lip that he spit on the pristine, white carpet.

"So you've taken up with the *lucani*. He seems strong enough to protect you. And the children."

Grace slid her grandmother a quick look. "That almost sounded like approval."

"Just an observation."

A growl from the other side of the room drew her attention away from Kaisie long enough to see that John and the two wolves, who she believed were Duke and Nic, had dealt with Ettore's two men. She had no idea if they were still alive and didn't care.

She wanted Ettore dead.

She got her wish a few seconds later.

Ettore hadn't stood a chance against Kaisie. With a final twist of his hands, Kaisie broke Ettore's neck and dropped his lifeless body to the floor.

She didn't wait for him to come to her. She ran for him, remembering at the last minute to drop the knife before she stabbed him with it.

Throwing her arms around his neck, she clung to him as his arms wrapped tight around her waist.

"Gods damn it, Grace. The next time I say stay put, I fucking mean it."

She laughed because his voice held absolutely no trace of anger. Just pure exasperation and relief. And his mouth, when he bent to kiss her, was hungry for hers.

When he finally let her up for air, he shook his head as he ran a shaking hand over her head. "Are you ready to go the hell home?"

"You're going to have to clean up your language, you know. You can't swear like that around the kids."

His smile made her light up. "Don't worry. They won't get any bad habits from me. You're the one with the temper."

Eyebrows raised, she opened her mouth to respond—

"Grace."

Her grandmother's voice totally ripped her out of the moment she'd been having with Kaisie and back into the reality of a room with at least one dead body and another two who would probably join him shortly.

She considered ignoring Graziella but knew her grandmother wouldn't let her get away with that.

Taking a deep, fortifying breath, she turned to face the woman who'd haunted her nightmares along with Ettore.

And realized her grandmother had lost some of her power to shock and awe her.

With Kaisie at her back, she looked Graziella in the eyes and waited.

Her grandmother raised one perfectly curved eyebrow at her.

"We need to talk."

"No, Grandmother. I don't think we do."

"Well, you can stick your head in the sand now but when I die, which won't be too long from now according to my doctors, I think you're going to want to understand a little bit about how this company works…since it will belong to you and your children."

Chapter Eight

Grace sat on Kaisie's screened porch, staring out into the dark.

Every now and then she'd see a shadow move through the underbrush. She knew the only reason she caught sight of the wolf was because he wanted her to.

The young soldier, Seth, was out there. She knew it was him. He'd come to the house earlier to tell her he'd be on patrol tonight.

She liked Seth. He didn't say much but he always had a smile for Alex and treated Amy like he did everyone else. He didn't talk much but when he had something to say, it was relevant and insightful. And he had the driest sense of humor, something they had in common.

The ride back to the den from the city had been quiet. The men hadn't had much to say and she had been too stunned from her grandmother's announcement to contribute to anything they might have said.

Her grandmother was dying. She was eighty-seven, so this wasn't a shock. Grace couldn't even muster up much sympathy because her grandmother had never shown her anything other than mild interest.

But Grace had been beyond shocked when her grandmother had dropped her bombshell this afternoon.

The only question Grace could ask was "Why?"

She continued to ask it even though her grandmother was still in New York and she was back in Pennsylvania. Where she planned to stay.

There was no way she was going to take control of her grandmother's company, not even to hold it in trust for her children. She didn't want anything to do with the *Mal*. She wanted to put all that behind her.

And yet…

The money from the company could fund her research into Alex's unknown disease and the *lucani* disease Dane Dimitriou was trying to cure. She could hire someone to run the company, which had been in her family for almost a hundred years, for her.

For that matter, she could give the reins over to her father, who was bound to be upset that his own mother had tossed him aside in favor of the daughter he'd barely spoken to in years.

"You don't have to make a decision tonight. You know that, right?"

She turned to find Kaisie watching her from the doorway. Her lips automatically curved in a smile at the sight of him leaning against the jamb.

Sexy just wasn't a strong enough word to describe what she thought of him. Long, lean, sleek. He made her heart pound just from one glance of those green eyes.

She couldn't believe how much she wanted him. Or how very much she loved him. It felt like a fever in her blood and she'd never thought that could be a good thing.

Now she wanted it to consume her.

She held out her hand and he smiled as he walked over to take it. And that fever became a raging bonfire.

Drawing in a deep breath, she caught the clean male scent of him and couldn't wait to take a bite out of the firm flesh of his chest. She couldn't imagine her life without him anymore.

And though that should have scared the life out of her, she felt nothing but absolute joy.

He grabbed her hand, lacing their fingers together then drawing her hand to his mouth. She thought he was going to kiss her but his tongue flicked out to paint her knuckles with heat.

She shivered and tugged on his hand but he refused to release her. "How much trouble are you in with Cole?"

Kaisie shrugged, as if it didn't matter that he'd disobeyed a direct order from his king and killed Ettore. "He understood, especially when I told him your grandmother gave us more than Marrucini ever would have."

"We can't be sure she doesn't have a hidden agenda. If the name she gave us is legitimate, she risked so much. I just can't believe she'd do that. You don't know her, Kaisie. She's not the type of person who would do that out of the goodness of her heart. The woman has no heart."

"I didn't smell a lie on her, babe. I seriously think she thinks she's telling the truth." He bent over to press his mouth against hers for a hard, heated kiss. "We don't know that Marrucini would've given us any more. At least now we have a place to start."

Staring into Kaisie's steady eyes, she wanted to believe her grandmother hadn't lied to them. That the information she'd given them about the leaders of the *Mal* was correct. But she knew her grandmother.

"Kaisie—"

He bent and pressed his lips against hers again, this time wrapping his arms around her and lifting her off the couch.

"Time for bed, babe."

She liked the sound of that. "But—"

"No buts." Another kiss.

Blessed Goddess, his kisses had the power to scramble her brain and leave her panting for him. "Are the kids asleep?"

Kaisie strode through the living room to his bedroom on the other side of the house. "Alex is. Amy's pretending to be and that's good enough for me."

"Kaisie…" She sighed as she nuzzled her nose against his neck. "I love you but you didn't sign up for this much crazy."

"Don't worry, baby." He kicked the door shut behind him. "I can handle crazy. I don't think I could handle losing you."

Tears welled and she didn't bother to blink them away. When he laid her on his bed and started to strip away her clothes, she watched him, seeing the heat in his eyes flare as he uncovered her.

He had her naked in seconds, his gaze sliding along her like a physical caress. Her nipples tightened, her thighs clenched and she could barely breathe, even though he did nothing more than stare at her.

When he finally met her gaze, she nearly combusted.

And when he tossed his shirt over his head and shucked his jeans down his legs, she felt her juices seep from her body.

He didn't make her wait any longer.

He fell on her with a hunger she returned, their mouths fused, their skin pressed tight. She slid a hand between them to wrap around his cock, hard and hot against her stomach. So silky.

Kaisie groaned and tore his mouth away to begin trailing kisses down her neck.

She knew he was headed toward her breasts and her nipples ached for the feel of his lips on them.

But she ached between her legs even more.

With one hand on his hip, she pushed and prodded until he complied with her silent demand.

The tip of his cock slid between her sensitive lower lips, filling her slowly and sensuously. She couldn't help the moan that escaped when he finally began to move.

With her arms wrapped around his shoulders, fingers sinking into the muscles of his back, she curled her legs around his hips and arched closer, taking him deeper.

"I love you." His breath rasped against her neck followed by a quick nip of her collarbone.

As he began to thrust, he took her mouth again and stole her breath.

He didn't let her up for air until she began to convulse around him. He rode her through her orgasm, pushing her higher, extending the sensation until her arms fell limp to the bed.

Only then did he release, the pulse of his orgasm making her breath hitch.

"Kaisie…"

"I know, babe." He pressed a kiss to her cheek. "You love me."

"Always."

Epilogue

"Push, Mara. That's it. The head's about to crown."

Struggling through the pain, Mara fought to keep her eyes open and on her cousin, Amy, as Amy translated the nurse Tamra's words into sign language.

Though she suspected her body would do whatever it wanted, she didn't want to do something wrong and hurt her child.

Behind her, Grace braced Mara's body with her own, her presence a comfort she couldn't acknowledge enough. Grace had been a godsend these last few weeks, steady, calm, the mother she'd always dreamed of having.

Now she was going to be a mother and—

Another contraction ripped through her abdomen and, though she heard herself scream in her head, no sound came out of her mouth. The *streghe* hadn't been able to release the spell. Yet.

She bore down, trying her damnedest to force her child from her body. Fear, joy and an almost tactile sense of anticipation crowded inside her.

What if—

Amy was signing. "The head's out. On the next contraction, push hard and you'll be able to hold your son."

Her son. Only hers. The *lucani* king had promised her. No one would take her child. No matter what.

Blessed Goddess, please—

Another agonizing contraction and she pushed and pushed until she thought she'd never be done and then, finally, the pressure eased.

She opened her eyes, desperate to see her baby. She caught sight of a tiny arm then a small body. The head. She needed to see his head.

At first glance, she couldn't see his face. Then she realized why.

It was covered with the caul. But not completely. The caul covered only a portion of his face.

She started to cry.

*****

Race didn't know what the hell he was doing here. It wasn't as if he was gonna go in there and…do something.

What the hell would he do? Mara probably wouldn't even want him there. Hell, he didn't know why he'd *want* to be in there. He only knew that when Kaisie had told him Mara was in labor, he'd had to come.

Six hours later, he'd done nothing more than pace like an expectant father. Which he wasn't. The baby wasn't his. Mara wasn't his.

Hell, most of the times they'd crossed paths since she'd been rescued from Florida, she'd barely looked at him.

He probably scared the shit out of her with all the tats and the body built for heavy-duty violence.

Beautiful, fragile, terrified, *pregnant* Mara didn't need him hanging around her, making her more anxious than she already was.

Vaffanculo, the girl had more than enough problems without his completely schizoid emotional reaction to her. She didn't need him following her around like an overgrown, lovesick hellhound.

He ran a hand over his head, the stubble softer than it had been just yesterday. He hadn't shaved it in a few weeks. Not since they'd gotten back from Florida. And no, he wasn't about to analyze why.

The murmur of voices from her room increased and he froze. Closing his eyes, he listened then heard the distinctive sound of a baby crying.

He ran for the door, stopping before he pushed it open.

Looking in the small window, his gaze immediately went to Mara.

Crying. Fuck, she was crying.

He had a hand on the door ready to push through. He didn't give a fuck what anyone else thought. He wanted in there and—

Her face totally transformed with a smile. A weepy, wet, totally exhausted smile that made his heart beat once again.

She reached out and Tam put a tiny, messy little body into Mara's arms.

Mara only had eyes for the baby but Race saw the pensive glances exchanged by Grace and Tam.

Shit. Just…shit.

Also by Stephanie Julian

eBooks:

Lucani Lovers 1: Kiss of Moonlight

Lucani Lovers 2: Moonlight Ménage

Lucani Lovers 3: Edge of Moonlight

Lucani Lovers 4: Moonlight Temptation

Lucani Lovers 5: Grace in Moonlight

Lucani Lovers 6: Shades of Moonlight

Magical Seduction 1: Seduced by Magic

Magical Seduction 2: Seduced in Shadow

Magical Seduction 3: Seduced and Ensnared

Magical Seduction 4: Seduced and Enchanted

Magical Seduction 5: Seduced by Chaos

Magical Seduction 6: Seduced by Danger

Magical Seduction 7: Seduced by Two

Size Matters

The Bigger They Are

Print Books:

Lucani Lovers 1: Kiss of Moonlight

Lucani Lovers 2: Moonlight Ménage

Lucani Lovers 3: Edge of Moonlight

Lucani Lovers 4: Moonlight Temptation

Magical Seduction 1 & 2: Shadow Magic

Magical Seduction 3 & 4: Ensnared and Enchanted

Magical Seduction 5 & 6: Chaos & Danger

About Stephanie Julian

Stephanie Julian is an avid reader who used to have a book-a-day habit. Then she realized she not only wanted to read books but write them, too. Romance has always been her first love, the sexier the better. Hot men, strong women and heaping helpings of magic dominate (and she does mean dominate) her blazing-hot stories.

When she's not writing, she's, well...she's certainly not cleaning. And she only cooks when her guys complain that they're hungry (ain't cereal grand!). Otherwise, she's got her fingers on a keyboard, her butt in a chair and her head in the stars.

The author welcomes comments from readers. You can find her website and email address on her author bio page at www.ellorascave.com.

Tell Us What You Think

We appreciate hearing reader opinions about our books. You can email us at Service@ellorascave.com (when contacting Customer Service, be sure to state the book title and author).

Why an electronic book?

We live in the Information Age—an exciting time in the history of human civilization, in which technology rules supreme and continues to progress in leaps and bounds every minute of every day. For a multitude of reasons, more and more avid literary fans are opting to purchase e-books instead of paper books. The question from those not yet initiated into the world of electronic reading is simply: *Why?*

1. ***Price.*** An electronic title at Ellora's Cave Publishing runs anywhere from 40% to 75% less than the cover price of the exact same title in paperback format. Why? Basic mathematics and cost. It is less expensive to publish an e-book (no paper and printing, no warehousing and shipping) than it is to publish a paperback, so the savings are passed along to the consumer.
2. ***Space.*** Running out of room in your house for your books? That is one worry you will never have with electronic books. For a low one-time cost, you can purchase a handheld device specifically designed for e-reading. Many e-readers have large, convenient screens for viewing. Better yet, hundreds of titles can be stored within your new library—on a single microchip. There are a variety of e-readers from different manufacturers. You can also read e-books on your PC or laptop computer. (Please note that Ellora's Cave does not endorse any specific brands.

You can check our website at www.ellorascave.com for information we make available to new consumers.)

3. *Mobility.* Because your new e-library consists of only a microchip within a small, easily transportable e-reader, your entire cache of books can be taken with you wherever you go.
4. *Personal Viewing Preferences.* Are the words you are currently reading too small? Too large? Too... ANNOYING? Paperback books cannot be modified according to personal preferences, but e-books can.
5. *Instant Gratification.* Is it the middle of the night and all the bookstores near you are closed? Are you tired of waiting days, sometimes weeks, for bookstores to ship the novels you bought? Ellora's Cave Publishing sells instantaneous downloads twenty-four hours a day, seven days a week, every day of the year. Our webstore is never closed. Our e-book delivery system is 100% automated, meaning your order is filled as soon as you pay for it.

Those are a few of the top reasons why electronic books are replacing paperbacks for many avid readers.

As always, Ellora's Cave welcomes your questions and comments. We invite you to email us at Service@ellorascave.com or write to us directly at Ellora's Cave Publishing Inc., 1056 Home Avenue, Akron, OH 44310-3502.

13036850R00107

Made in the USA
San Bernardino, CA
06 July 2014